Return to Side Lake

THE TURTLE CREEK SERIES
BOOK THREE

JENNIFER WALTERS

Return to Side Lake

Jennifer Walters

****

For my daughter, Sidney

Other books by Jennifer Walters

The Fredrickson's Series

Always Right Here
Northern Winds
Greenrock Road

The Turtle Creek Series

The Memories We Keep
A Side Lake Summer
Return to Side Lake

Standalone

The Weight of Change

www.JenniferWaltersAuthor.com

****

One

Kat

Her knuckles clenched the steering wheel at ten and two, when the Maps app went off telling her to take a right ahead instead of a left. She tried to find the lane to turn, but instead a giant mining hole replaced the familiar turn that took her to highway five. It looked like a crater, not a manmade hole for mining iron ore. Sure, it was beautiful, but the crater was way too close to the highway.

Where was the turnoff to highway five? She felt so lost. Everything looked so different since she left the Iron Range years ago. She turned into Chisholm and took a left on the unfamiliar roundabout.

Stupid detour.

She kept driving. Not to mention she was so annoyed she had to drive all the way through Chisholm just to get to the road that led to Side Lake, adding more time to the already long trip. She had been driving three hours, and she still wondered why she even came. She hated this place, and she had promised herself she would never come back, ever. But here she was.

How was she supposed to feel about being back in Side Lake after all these years? And where was she going when she got there? When her aunt called and broke the news, her mother had died she threw some stuff in a bag, unsure of how long she would be gone, and she left right away. No thinking involved, her body just reacted before she had a second to process it.

She often thought about her mother passing and how she would be happy when it happened one day. That all her troubles would be solved. Then why was she acting all crazy and numb when it actually happened? And all she could think about was getting in her car and getting to Side Lake as fast as she could. Why did it feel like her lungs were deflated and she struggled just to breathe? It felt nothing like relief, not one bit.

Her mother left the house to her, which was surprising since she was the one who shipped her across the state fifteen years ago just to get rid of her. She had no interest in the house or her mother's money. Just the thought of going into her mother's house made her lungs heavy.

She wasn't feeling the country music that way playing on the local radio station, so she turned the dial until Metallica came on.

"Good." She turned up the volume to the point of hurting her ears. She screamed with the song as the tears finally flowed uncontrollably.

She turned the volume even higher to cover the sound of her own sobbing. She screamed the song and cried, releasing the burning in her lungs and gut. Theo n reasonable explanation for what she was doing. She was acting crazy, but it didn't matter. Nothing made any sense to her about the way she was acting. The song ended and as if on cue, so did the tears. She sniffled, wiped her eyes, and cleared her throat. flipped down her visor and wiped off the mascara streaks on her cheeks and blinked away the tears.

She looked at her phone, four bars. Her hands shook, but she was able to find Lyndsey's name in her phone and push call. She turned the corner onto Greenrock Road as the ringing stopped.

Someone answered, but the voice was deep. She pulled the phone away from her ear to make sure she called Lyndsey.

"Hi, Kat. It's Kevin Finney here. Long time, no see."

Her face scrunched up, and a sob escaped before she could stop it. She was glad Kevin was with Lyndsey but this was not the time for him to joke around and chat with her. She needed her friend. Were they together now? Why did he have Lyndsey's phone, anyway? She heard her friend's voice in the background.

She let out a sob. "Kevin, I'm sorry but I need to talk to Lyndsey. Is she there?"

The phone spit static on the other end and then Lyndsey answered. "I'm here, Kat. Are you okay?"

The phone beeped and went quiet. The call dropped. She pulled into Lyndsey's driveway and called again, with no success. She ran to the door, but it was locked so she made her way to the other side of her friend's house and spotted Lyndsey.

"Kat, you're here? What are you doing here? I thought you'd never come back. Are you okay?" Lyndsey's voice quivered the way Kat's whole body felt.

"I told you I'd come back over my mother's dead body and guess what?" Only Lyndsey could understand her dark humor.

"Oh, Kat! I'm so sorry." She ran to her, and they cried in

each other's arms. As they separated, Lyndsey looked over her shoulder at Kevin.

Kat wiped her tears away. "Here we are again. She's my best friend, Kevin. I thought I told you to back off years ago."

He looked the same as he had the last time she saw him, only a few more lines around the eyes. He was still just as handsome. Were they back together after all these years? She could not bring herself to ask. This was all too much, just being back here.

Lyndsey had never mentioned her and Kevin were actually together now, and that hurt a bit. Living across the state from her had put a distance between them even though they kept in touch. Long distance friendships were not the same as being together.

"It's great to see you again, too, Kat meow. If only Ethan was here."

Kat wiped her eyes and laughed. Thank goodness Ethan was no longer in the area. Last she heard he was living somewhere in New York City. "I'm pretty sure he isn't living in Minnesota anymore. I don't think I would recognize him if I saw him."

"About that," Lyndsey said with a nervous smile. "Ethan's back."

Kat's swollen eyes widened, and her chin dropped. "He's here?"

"Well, not here as in at my house, but he's staying at Pine Beach."

She could not believe her ears. The past was repeating itself. "In a motor home? Like a permanent camper?"

Kevin shook his head and answered before Lyndsey had a chance. "No, no, in a cabin. I'm sorry, I thought you knew he was back in town." He put his hand on her shoulder and then pulled her in for a hug. "I'm going to let the two of you talk.

I'm so sorry about your mom. I know you two weren't close. I know all too well, but I'm sure it still hurts."

He smiled at her, and she forced a smile back through the tears. "It's okay. Thanks, Kev. It's great seeing you. Hopefully, the next time I see you I'm not such a hot mess."

Once he shut the door, Lyndsey turned to Kat. "Come with me." She led her to the porch swing they spent so much time on as children. They both sat down.

"How are you doing? What happened to your mother?"

Before she answered, Kevin came out and handed them water bottles and a box of tissues. He nodded with a sympathetic look and went back inside.

"Wow, that was so thoughtful. I was not expecting Kevin to answer your phone. I'll tell you, it sure threw me off. Why didn't you tell me?"

Lyndsey did not fight the sudden change in subject. Instead, she said, "It all just happened so fast. I didn't want to jinx it. You know our history, it always seemed like something —or someone got in the way. But I think this time it's different."

"I'm so happy for you." She meant it. Lyndsey deserved happiness, and she always knew they were meant to be together. But she could not feel their happiness right now, not like a good friend should. Her body was too numb. "Is it just me or has he gotten even hotter after all these years?"

Lyndsey smiled, her entire face lighting up at the mention of Kevin. Then her expression changed.

She placed a hand on Kat's forearm. "We'll talk about him later. I want to talk about you. You're here, in Side Lake. You never wanted to come back. Are you okay?"

Kat nodded and turned her head away. She replayed it repeatedly in her mind. The call from her aunt, the drive here she hardly remembered, packing her bag without thinking at all. Was that hours ago? It felt like minutes ago and weeks ago at the same time.

Her eyelids were heavy, and she struggled to keep them open.

"Aunt Bev called. I could barely understand her as she struggled to tell me the news. It was almost like a dream. She said my mom had an aneurism. Not only was it sudden but they believe she died in her sleep. I guess she had some heart issues I never knew about. But I don't know why it hurts so much. I hated her."

"Oh, honey. She is your mom. Of course it hurts. She hurt you and shipped you away so she didn't have to deal with you, but that doesn't mean you didn't love her deep down."

"It makes little sense. What she did to me was unforgivable. She never apologized after all these years."

"Kevin went through the same thing when his dad died. He told me it hurt so bad, but he struggled to tell anyone because he felt like he shouldn't care that his father died after all the terrible things he did to his family. He wanted him to disappear for so long and when he finally did, he didn't feel relief. It was so strange to him."

"Yeah. My mom abandoned me and here I was racing to Side Lake as if I thought she might still be here, and I wanted to see her. Maybe I just wanted to make sure she was really gone. I'm a terrible person."

"You aren't terrible. She hurt you."

"I'm pretty sure I drove eighty the whole way here. I don't even remember to be honest."

Lyndsey laughed, "You're lucky you made it here alive and without a ticket."

"God owes me," she said. "But let's talk about something else. What happened with you and Kevin?"

Lyndsey wiped a tear off Kat's cheek before looking over

her shoulder, as if making sure Kevin hadn't suddenly appeared out of thin air.

"I told you Kevin's ex-wife, Tracey, lied about someone burglarizing her house in a sad attempt to get Kevin back, right?"

"Yes, but that's the last I heard about it."

"Well, after she admitted to pinning everything on me in college and causing Kevin and I to fight all those years, she was arrested. Kevin showed up at my door and apologized for everything. We've been hanging out ever since. It's as if we got a redo and all that stuff never happened."

Lyndsey's smile widened, and her eyes filled with excitement. "I can't believe I'm saying this aloud, but I am pretty sure I'm in love with him, and I want to spend the rest of my life with Kevin because I can't imagine life without him."

"Wow, Lyndsey, I mean you've known him long enough. If it were anyone else, I'd say you're moving too fast, but I always knew the two of you were meant to be. I'm so happy for you. Is he living here with you?"

She shook her head but did not seem certain. "No, he still has a house in town, but he knows I love it when he's here. We're in a good place."

"I'm so happy for you." She swallowed a giggle. "I don't know why, but I'd like to meet Tracey. I've heard so much about her all these years."

Lyndsey lifted her eyebrow. "No, you don't. Trust me. Hopefully, they lose the key to her cell."

They both laughed.

"Where's your boyfriend, Andy, right?"

"He had to work, and I guess I needed to do this on my own."

Lyndsey looked at her sideways.

"He wanted to come. I was in shock, and I just left. I did text him."

7

"It's as if everything has changed in the past fifteen years in Side Lake and also as if nothing has changed at all."

"Quit changing the subject. You sure sound like Kevin when he first came back to the lake after not coming here for a few years. A lot of memories."

"Yeah." The bad ones overpowered all the good ones in her head.

They sat in silence listening to the sound of the boat waves hitting the shore and staring at the beautiful lake before them.

"Do you want to stay here tonight or are you planning on staying at your mom's?"

Going into that house alone was too horrible to contemplate. "I would love to stay here. I think I need a good night sleep before I face all the memories within those walls."

Lyndsey squeezed her hand. "You're welcome to stay as long as you want."

"Thanks. So, Ethan is really back in Side Lake?"

"Yes, he is. Is there a part of you that wants to see him again?"

"No." The word snapped. "I'm so sorry, that came out wrong. I don't want him to know I'm here. We didn't exactly end on good terms."

Good terms, that was a laugh. She hated him. He never tried to find her after she left. She dreamed he'd find her and tell her how much he loved her after she moved, but he never did. Proof he never really cared about her at all. "Please tell Kevin not to tell Troy or Troy will tell Victoria and she'll tell Ethan and—"

Lyndsey opened a bottle of water. "I get it. But he may find out because the whole town will be talking about your mother. Everyone in Side Lake knows her. She was part of the coffee crowd that went down to the Side Lake Store every Thursday morning, you know."

"I don't understand why they liked her. She was a horrible person."

Lyndsey shrugged. "She was different with them. I think they knew how she could get, but she got better over the years. The ladies here are so kind and forgiving, I'm sure you know that."

She did, but would they like her anymore. She avoided them all for so long.

Lyndsey squeezed her hand. "I'm so glad you're here, for however long that may be. I've missed you."

Kat stood up, and Lyndsey followed. "I've missed you, too. Thank you for being the person I could come to. You've always been like a sister to me, even if we haven't lived on the same side of the state for like fifteen years."

"Always. I'm glad you feel that way. You would do the same, you know." Lyndsey led the way inside. "Are you hungry at all?"

"No. I'm exhausted. Would you mind if I sneak off to bed? Is that rude since I just got here?"

Lyndsey waved her off. "Are you kidding me? You've had a very long day, I'd think you were lying if you said you weren't exhausted. Let me show you to Brad's old room, which is now my guest bedroom. Available at your convenience."

Without Lyndsey, she wasn't sure she would have been brave enough to come back to Side Lake and face this place alone. No matter how much time passed, it was as if nothing ever changed between them. She was a once in a lifetime friend.

Two

Ethan

Ethan woke to the smell of cedar and coffee, and the brightness of the sun rising and shining in through his window. He blinked until he remembered where he was. Side Lake. He jumped up and poured himself a cup of coffee.

The busyness of his life in Manhattan was exhausting, and he always felt rushed. Here in Side Lake, he felt relaxed and well-rested. He had so many wonderful memories and only a few he did not care to remember, such as losing the girl he fell in love with as a teenager.

Every summer, his family would pack up and head to Side Lake to camp in their motor home that was parked at a permanent location. He made friends at the resort, which was its own community, and he spent the summers swimming and wake boarding on the lake. He loved living the small city life as a child with nature all around him.

Just after he finished college, his parents stopped coming to the lake. Only Ethan's sister, Victoria, continued to spend her summers at their camper. She had been dating Troy

Finney, and they stayed in the camper together in the summers until she got her fancy job. They now spent their summers traveling all over the world for work.

He and Victoria were both writers, only his sister wrote travel blogs, and he wrote romance novels. Best-selling romance novels under a pen name. He decided not to write under his name when he submitted his first book to agents in case he failed. He was also told romance books written by women were more popular compared to those written by men. He wanted to hide behind someone else's name so the rejections would not feel so real. He certainly got a lot of rejection letters, and he thought he would never make it, but then an offer letter arrived and everything moved fast after that. He had five best sellers before his writing slipped and writer's block took over his brain.

He struggled with inspiration the longer he was away from the lake. He lived on a river in Manhattan, but that was not the same. Life was fast-paced, and more famous authors who wrote more bestsellers than he ever could surrounded him. He felt small and intimidated, leaving him with imposter syndrome and comparitinitus.

His computer sat on the desk in front of the window over-looking the lake. He placed his hands on the keyboard and the words flowed for two hours straight. His mind had relaxed enough to break through the barriers in his head.

At nine in the morning, he finally took a break and changed his clothes for a run.

His shoes bounced off the gravel roads in the quiet resort, the sound echoing all around him. Once he turned onto the road, the sound of his shoes on the pavement became less irri-tating and more meditative. The air was already muggy, and the sun was beating down on him. Minnesota was hot and humid in the summer and brutally cold in the winter. And full of mosquitoes in the summer, but they only bothered him when he stopped running.

He made his way toward Bimbo's Octagon, the only restaurant on the chain of lakes accessible by boat. He stopped to catch his breath and walked up the dock to stare out at the lake. The water was clean and beautiful, and the air free of smog and debris. A perfect day.

A bald eagle landed on a huge nest in the trees along the shoreline. Another sign of nature along Side Lake. He closed his eyes and took a deep breath. A nice long run to Turtle Creek Road would be a good idea.

By the time he reached the familiar road, he was exhausted from the heat and dehydrated with no water. He was relieved when he spotted Kevin outside, mowing Lyndsey's lawn.

Kevin saw him and let go of the lever on his mower. "Ethan, buddy, so great to see you. Lyndsey said you were here. Aren't you dying running in this heat?"

Ethan leaned over, resting his hands on his knees, he struggled to catch his breath. He tried to speak but his mouth was dry. "Can I trouble you for some water?"

"Of course, come on in. Lyndsey will be bummed she missed you. She should be back soon. She went with Whitney and Maddy to town for some groceries," he said, while walking through the house and grabbing Ethan a large glass of water.

Ethan held out his hand to retrieve it, water never looked so good. He downed the cool drink and sighed..

"I like to run later in the night when it cools off, not in the heat of the day. You are brave," Kevin said.

"Brave or stupid, one of the two anyway."

Kevin laughed. "Do you have plans tonight? We should have a couple drinks, maybe some dinner and catch up?"

"Yeah. You aren't working tonight?"

"I'm on my six days off stretch, and Lyndsey is planning on helping Kat go through her mother's stuff."

He paused the glass halfway to his mouth. "Kat? She's in town? What is she doing in Side Lake?"

Kevin's face turned red, which was rare for a police officer. Ethan knew right away Kevin wished he could take back his words. What was he hiding?

"I have such a big mouth..." He nervously ran his fingers through his hair. "Listen, Lyndsey and Kat would both kill me if they knew I told you."

"Told me what?" He was so confused.

"Kat's mother passed away, and she's here cleaning up her mother's house to sell it or rent it, or something like that. I'm not sure she's decided what she's doing with it yet. She's having a hard time with it all."

Kat was back in Side Lake? He never thought that would happen. She stayed as far away from the place as she could from what Troy told him. Although now that her mother was gone she had no reason to fear this place.

"She really doesn't want to see me, huh? She's the one who left me a Dear John letter and I'm the jerk?" He shook his head.

"I'm sorry, man. I'm no expert on women."

"How did she know I was here?"

A guilty look crossed Kevin's face as he ran his hand through his hair again.

"Kevin?"

"Look, she knows you're staying at Pine Beach, but she's upset right now. The timing isn't the best. And the two of you haven't spoken since you were teenagers."

She was holding a grudge for something that ended many years ago, not by his choice. This was not on him, but he would not confront her. He'd be a jerk to bring this up when her mother just died, even if she hated her mother.

"You need to be the better person here. Go to the funeral with me and pay your respects."

"For the woman that hated me and drove my childhood sweetheart out of town and out of my life?"

"Yes. The woman is gone, Ethan. What does it matter? It will be good for you to see Kat. Maybe clear the air?"

They walked outside, and Ethan leaned against the garage. Did he want to see Kat? She broke his heart and never looked back.

"Do you want a ride back? I've seen what heatstroke does to people, and I don't want to take a trip to the ER today because you ran when it's eighty-five degrees out with ninety-five percent humidity."

He patted Kevin's back as he walked past him. "Don't worry, I'll walk. Take your own advice." He pointed at the lawn mower. Kevin smiled and saluted him before he bent over to jerk the pull-start.

Ethan shook his head and grinned at his friend before he walked away. Same old Kevin.

He walked down the road and stopped at the end of Kat's long driveway. The night he ran out of her house in a panic circled in his mind. The memory of Kat's mother throwing pillows at him when she caught them having sex made him laugh out loud. He never ran so fast. He hated leaving Kat there, but she pushed him out the door, a look of panic in her eyes. She was terrified of her mother, and he soon found out her fear was justified.

Their relationship was short-lived, and Kat's mother did not allow him to come over again. But he never stopped thinking about Kat after all these years. He tried dating, but no one compared. When Lyndsey delivered the Dear John letter, he was crushed. But he yearned to know what happened to Kat. He tried to hunt her down but came up empty. He wrote her letters that were never answered. Her mother probably never gave them to her. He had no way of finding Kat but he tried everything he could to track her down.

He was still angry at Kat for what she did, but he had no choice. She never tried to reach out to him after all these years to explain more than just what was in the letter she left him. Now she wanted her return kept secret from him? His blood boiled at the thought. What did he do? He had no choice. She made sure of that long ago.

His phone vibrated. His agent was calling. He picked up and continued walking down the gravel road.

"Zoey, what did you think?" He held his breath to wait for her reaction.

"Ethan, it's brilliant! It's so much like your old stuff. That lake life is good for you, you know that?"

"I do. That's why I'm here. It's as if I can't stop writing. The words are just pouring out of me." His agent was ready to drop him before he came back. He had struggled to write like he did back when the lake, the pureness of nature, and the lake people were fresh on his mind.

"I'm so glad to hear that. Keep writing and send me some more pages by the end of the week. You keep this up and publishers will fight for this book."

He felt the characters come to life here. He had found his inspiration again.

"And Ethan, you need to get ready to announce who you are to the world. The book tours are going to be unavoidable. I've even pitched this book to a movie producer. Keep these pages coming. I'm so relieved you found your mojo again."

He did not want to think about everyone finding out his secret. Who he really was. He wanted to blend in, not stick out. He needed to talk to Victoria, she would know what to do. She was the only one who knew his secret. She told no one, not even Troy, and swore she never would. Kevin and Troy were brothers, but Troy had a big mouth. If he found out, everyone would know, and he did not want that to happen.

He pushed the nervous thinking out of his head as he walked up the road to Pine Beach, the place that felt like home.

Sweat rings formed on his chest and under his arms. Right now all he needed was to dive into the beautiful lake in front of him.

He threw his shirt on the light sandy beach and removed his shoes and socks. He ran into the water as fast as he could, then he dove under. The refreshing coolness of a clean lake calmed him down. As a swimmer in high school, the familiar feeling of the cold water against his body reminded him of his happy place. Noise did not reach under water, and he was free from all his troubles for just a moment. Being alone with his thoughts and his dreams brought him joy until he resurfaced and made his way back to the shore and faced it all.

Three

Kat

The dumpster was already in her driveway when she reached her mother's house. It was hard to believe this house was no longer her mother's, it was hers, there was not even a mortgage. Her aunt told her that her mother left her some money, too, but she couldn't care less. She would rather give all her mother's money away than to think about her every time she spent even a dime of her mother's money.

She stood on the back deck, looking over the lake. Her house was the only one on the peninsula. The house was breathtaking but a little too large and showy for her taste. Mainly, it reminded her that money was more important to her mother than she was.

She took her time going into the house. Part of her worried the interior would be different than she remembered, but the other part of her worried it would be exactly the same as when she left.

"Well, here goes nothing." She took a deep breath and tapped in the code. The door beeped, and the light turned green. She turned the knob and stepped inside.

White marble tiles covered the floor on the main level, and the living room and dining room had white carpet that ran all the way up the stairs and throughout all the rooms. The living room walls comprised floral wallpaper that brightened the living room walls, along with the turquoise furniture.

The house was immaculate. Her mother always made sure everything had a place, and everything was to be put back in its place immediately. Maroon pillows were set perfectly fluffed on the couch, and the brick fireplace was neat as if it was just dusted and never used. A floor to ceiling bookshelf lined the far wall. Her favorite part of her mother's house was the living room where the wall shelving was filled with books of all genres.

She ran her fingers along the books and checked for dust. Not a speck. That was one thing her and her mother had in common, their passion for reading and collecting books. A recent addition to the bookshelves was a sliding ladder, which reminded her of Belle's library in *Beauty and the Beast*. She was unsure when her mother added the ladder, but she had to admit it was exactly what this room needed.

She eyed the complete collection of Elizabeth Conrad books. She did not know her mother was an Elizabeth Conrad fan, but she too had all her books. They were more alike than she thought and she wasn't sure how she felt about that.

She made her way to the floor to ceiling windows and the cushion in the window seat that her mother converted into a reading nook. She sat down, feeling a bit overwhelmed just being back in this house after all these years.

She could see herself living here, reading all these books as she lay on the reading nook by the window in the winter with the fireplace warming her up, a small Afghan her grandmother crocheted draped across her lap.

But all the terrible memories of her mother erased this vision from her mind as quickly as it came on. Like the time her mother screamed at her for not doing the dishes, which ended with her mother throwing a vase that almost hit Kat between the eyes. Luckily, she ducked just in time. The vase crashed against the wall behind her. Or the time her mother slapped her across the face for eating the last banana.

Her mother was evil and abusive and controlling, and she ruined Kat. She shipped her off at the first sight of trouble, not just once but twice. She could never forgive her, and her mother never even cared enough to try. The question Kat struggled with was if her mother hated her so much, why leave everything she had to her? Maybe it was because she had no one else. Maybe it was because she was continuing to manipulate the town after she left by making them all think how great she was to leave everything to the daughter that disowned her. She imagined that was probably what they all thought. Her mother had a way of making people see what she wanted them to see.

Break over, she had to clean this place out so she could get out of town as fast as she could.

She made her way into the kitchen, the walls and countertops decorated in a fruit theme. An apple boarder ran along the ceiling, the same as it had been since Kat was a little girl. The stove and butcher block stood in the middle of the floor, a perfect place for preparing dinner. A light shone down from the ceiling. Nothing had changed in the kitchen since the day she left.

A memory of her mother in the kitchen making an apple pie and letting her help roll out the crust came back. She had some good memories of her mother, but once she got older, her mother changed. She became mean and controlling, and no longer cared to listen to a word Kat had to say.

Upstairs, she paid attention to the white carpet that ran through every room. Not one stain. Not even a small stain or discoloration.

She went into the master bedroom and jumped on the bed. Because she could. If her mother could see her jumping on her bed, she would be pissed. The thought made her jump even higher and land even harder. She jumped off the bed after finally losing her breath to check out the bathroom attached to the master bedroom.

The huge jacuzzi tub took up most of the bathroom and the large windows were directly in front of the tub so she could take a nice bubble bath and look out at the lake. Her mother never let her bathe in the tub when she was growing up. It was time to do what she wanted. This was now her house. She may sell it, but not today. She would be here at least a week, going through all her mother's storage and packing up the house. Selling the house would be easy since it was surrounded by lakeshore on all three sides and secluded from the other cabins and houses on Turtle Creek Road.

Back downstairs, she made her way through the gazebo. She smiled at the thought of that memorable night with Ethan. The look on her mother's face as she walked in on them.

Outside, she looked down the three sets of stairs that led to the long dock. Lilies and weeds grew alongside the dock because her mother no longer had a boat on the lake to disturb them. Putting the boat in and taking it out each fall and spring was probably too much work for her mother when no one was using the boat, anyway. Kat's aunt no longer came to visit her mother after Kat was banished and sent to live with her. Her aunt was kind and continued to keep in touch with her mother, even though she treated her terribly.

She stared out at the lake and took a deep breath of the fresh air. Being back in Side Lake was much different from living in a big city. She missed the calmness of the water, long days relaxing at the lake, and bonfires at night with her friends.

Tears flowed down her cheeks, and her vision blurred. When was the last time she cried before coming back? She could not remember. This was three times in two days now. Why? She blocked out her emotions so she would never be vulnerable again and here she was, unable to turn off the faucet of emotions.

She made her way inside and down the stairs to the basement. She would start down there and make her way upstairs. First the sauna. She opened the door and took a deep breath. The aroma of cedar wood made her want to stay in there forever and breathe it in. But no, she had to pack up the house and return to her home far away from this place.

She opened the storage closet and, of course, everything was neatly stored in plastic bins. She took the top off the first one, packed full of holiday decorations. After she wrote donate on the side, she moved it to the far wall.

The next bin was labeled Katrina. She did not know her mother kept a bin of her stuff. She had yet to go into her childhood room, so maybe her mother packed up all her stuff and put it away so she didn't have to think about her anymore.

On the top were baby clothes, some papers from school, and some of her favorite books from her teenage years. She was about to open a photo album when the doorbell rang.

Who even knew she was here? She checked her phone, no message from Lyndsey that she was coming over. Who could it be? She ran up the stairs and peeked out the window. Lyndsey stared back at her. She opened the door.

"What are you doing here? You should have texted me."

Lyndsey pushed past her. "I know, but if I asked if I could come help you, you would just tell me no, and I figured you needed some support today. You've always been terrible at asking for help. And I'm your best friend. I'm sorry, but this is what best friends do."

Kat laughed and hugged her. How could she be mad when she cared enough to show up?

"Wow, her house looks exactly the same as when we are kids. Is it weird being back here?"

"Yes."

Kat grabbed a bottle of wine from inside the fridge and the bottle opener out of the drawer.

"Look at you. You still know your way around this kitchen after all these years."

"Yeah, my mom didn't like change."

Lyndsey eyed the room. "Yeah, I'd say. Other than the gorgeous new library and ladder over there. Did you find anything weird you wish you never found yet?"

"Weird?"

"Yeah, you know people always have secrets hidden in their house they don't think anyone will ever see."

"Funny you say that because I found a bin with my name on it, which is weird. I never thought she cared enough to keep anything of mine."

Kat poured a glass for Lyndsey. They both took a drink.

Lyndsey put the glass down on the table. "What was in it?"

"Just a bunch of stuff from my childhood."

"Hmm. That sounds normal. I mean, you know she loved you, right?"

Kat grunted. "I don't know if I'd go that far."

"Come on, she held onto stuff from your childhood. She probably thought the two of you would reconnect one day. It's her loss. She missed out on a wonderful, caring daughter. That's on her."

Kat took another drink. "I am pretty great," she said with a hint of sarcasm .

"Damn right you are, and she missed it." Lyndsey sighed. "She was so young for a brain aneurism. Probably thought she had more time to reconcile."

"I doubt she ever would."

"Well, maybe you'll find some closure when you go through her stuff."

She thought about that. What could she find in this house that would help her forgive her mother? Nothing could undue all the pain her mother had caused her over the years.

She put her wine down and looked at Lyndsey. "Can I ask you a question?"

Lyndsey blinked. "Anything. What's on your mind?"

"That day I gave you the letter for Ethan before I left for good—"

"No, I did not read it."

She had forgotten how in-tuned they always were with each other's thoughts. How Lyndsey could read her mind. She missed having Lyndsey in her every day-to-day life.

Would she lose Lyndsey when she found out the truth? The secrets she'd hidden from her all these years. Secrets that would most likely ruin their friendship.

"Why? What was in that letter? I've always wondered."

Kat shook her head. "I can't believe you never read the letter."

Lyndsey put her glass up to her lips. "You told me not to. I promised."

"I'm not sure I would have done the same," Kat said with a laugh. She wanted to avoid answering the question as long as possible.

"Yeah, you would have. I have a question for you."

"Shoot."

"Do you want to go to dinner tonight at Riverside?"

She considered it, but going anywhere was a struggle for her today. She was nowhere near ready to face the town. It was enough just having to be at the funeral with all the people talking about her mother.

"Before you answer, I want you to know Kevin and Ethan are going there. It may be nice to see him, say hello? Forgive him for whatever happened between the two of you all those years ago?"

"No!" The word exploded out of her with more vehemence than she meant. "I'm sorry, I'd rather not. I'm too busy, anyway. I have to write the obituary for my mother, and my aunt is coming over tomorrow morning to help me plan the funeral. I don't want to see anyone before the funeral. Everyone will tell me how sorry they are or asking where I have been all these years. Why I never visit. Ugh, this funeral is going to be horrible."

She felt the tears forming, and she blinked fast to hold back the blurriness. If she started crying, she might not be able to stop.

"I'll be right there by your side, and I'll tell them to back off. It's none of their business, anyway," Lyndsey said with a smile. "Do you need any help to plan the funeral?"

Kat shook her head. "My aunt did most of it. She offered, and all I had to do was the obituary."

"That's a relief."

"Yeah."

Lyndsey would give her the shirt of her back if she asked. If only she could return the favor and be honest and tell her the truth about what happened all those years ago. She owed her that. After the funeral, she would tell her the truth, even if the truth ended their friendship. It was time to get it all off her chest and be honest once and for all.

Four

Ethan

Kevin was sitting at a high table when he walked in. Riverside was packed full of a few locals, but mainly summer people.

"Hey, buddy. I ordered you a beer."

Ethan picked up a menu and sat down, taking a drink of his beer. "Thanks, man. I'm starving. Have you ordered anything yet?"

"Nope, but here comes the server if you're ready."

The waitress took both their orders.

"So, what's new with you? How long are you back for?" Kevin asked. "Last time I saw you was my brother and your sister's wedding."

"That was one hell of a wedding," he said. It was a wedding he would never forget. The bridal party came in on boats and Side Lake was the theme of the beach wedding.

"I still wonder if they had a backup plan in case it rained.

They had to be glued to that weather app until the morning of."

Ethan laughed. "I believe Victoria's backup plan was if it rained nothing would change, but if lightning struck, they'd just elope."

He nodded. "That sounds like them."

"You seemed a bit preoccupied at the wedding," Ethan said with a smirk.

"Yeah, I was too busy trying to impress my girl."

Ethan's eyebrows raised. "It's about time. Did the two of you ever hook up when you were teenagers? I always knew you would end up together."

"No, but we kissed once. I was stupid and let my hormones lead me in other directions. Man, I was stupid back then."

Ethan nodded. "Me too." He shook his head at the thought of Kat. "I still can't believe my sister ended up marrying your brother."

"Yeah, small world. He's whipped," he said with a laugh. "I never thought my brother would get married, but he's genuinely happy. Troy treats Victoria like a princess."

"They're happy traveling the world together. Must be nice," Ethan said dryly.

"How about you? What's new?"

He hated this question. His career was a secret, nor could he remember the last time he was in a relationship. He had to tread lightly. "I'm just living here for a few months, hoping to relax and enjoy nature. It's a nice change from the busyness of my normal life. I'm able to work remotely, so why not?"

"Any women in your life? Kevin didn't make eye contact when he asked.

This was not a normal Kevin question, and he had an idea where it came from. "No women in my life at the moment."

. . .

Without a doubt, Lyndsey was trying to get Kat and him back on good terms. Hoping they would end up together like they used to be. A reason to get Kat to stay and not move back to the cities.

The waitress brought them their burgers and another beer for each of them. Ethan looked up at the canoe hanging from the ceiling. The whole restaurant had been remodeled, and the canoe added a unique touch that could only be pulled off at a woodsy restaurant like this one.

"So, does Kat know you're here with me tonight?"

"I'm sure Lyndsey told her. Are you planning on going to the funeral?"

He looked up from his food. "Does she not want me to?"

Kevin shook his head. "It's a funeral. Half of Side Lake will be there. She's not admitting it, but I think Kat wants you to show up. I'm not sure why she's upset with you, but it's about time you found out. The two of you need to make up, and the only way that is going to happen is if you apologize and put this all behind you."

"What?" Ethan rolled his eyes. "That sounds like something Lyndsey would say, not you."

"Okay, fine. Guilty."

Ethan leaned forward and took a bite of his burger. "I don't think a funeral is the best place to win her over, and I don't even know if I want to. I also don't know if she would want me there in the first place."

He had no doubt her mother's funeral was not the best place for their reunion, especially when she was still angry with him after all these years. He'd like to set that straight with her another time.

"I'm just saying Kat can be a bit stubborn. The only way she's going to see you is if you're at her mother's funeral. She can't kick you out, and you can be there for a shoulder for her to lean on."

"You know Lyndsey would kill you if she heard you saying that about Kat."

He shrugged. "I don't care. It's true, and I want you around more while you're here, and Lyndsey and I think you and Kat had some unresolved issues you need to put behind you. Don't get me wrong, I'm not saying you will pick up where you were when she left or anything."

Where exactly was that? Did Kevin know about the letter? Did Lyndsey read it that day? If not, maybe Kat told her after all these years what it said and she told Kevin. Either way, he wanted to talk to Kat alone and find out what had happened. Not knowing for sure haunted him.

He had enough secrets just hiding his writing career from his friends, family, and his readers. He wanted to clear the air between them, but that was on her. He wanted to see her, but not because he still had feelings for her. He was past all that, but he could not help but wonder if they still had a connection or if that was just teenage lust.

"I'd like to hang out with you guys more while I'm here, too," Ethan said. "We were so close back then, and it would be great to have everyone together again, even for a short time. Since Troy and my sister are thinking about moving into your parents' place, the entire gang would be here."

"Don't forget Brad. Then again, none of us liked him when we were kids."

"What's he like now? Is he still living around here? I saw him at the wedding, but we didn't have a chance to talk."

"Ah, man, your sister didn't tell you?"

"Tell me what?"

"He lives a couple of doors down from Lyndsey. His daughter was killed in a car accident and he and his wife, Maddy, got divorced. He's had it rough."

Ethan shook his head at the sadness of it all. "Oh man, that's terrible."

"They did end up back together, and they had another kid. A little boy. Oh, and they got married again."

"Geez, no joke, huh? That's a lot to wrap my brain around. Now I feel like an ass judging him for the way he was when we were young. Are he and Lyndsey close?"

Kevin took the last bite of his burger and put his napkin on his plate. "Oh yeah, she's even closer to his wife. He's good people now. Not such a jackass." Kevin laughed and drank the rest of his beer. "Although he got into a fight with a teacher at the school, he works at. The teacher kicked his ass."

"I'm glad to hear that. He lives on Turtle Creek Road. Does everyone live on that road?"

"Pretty much. Except you, of course."

Ethan pulled up at Lyndsey's house early the next morning. He was picking up Kevin for the funeral, since Lyndsey would be riding with Kat.

He grinned. Kevin's not too subtle way of making sure he went to the funeral because, for some reason, Kevin and Lyndsey thought this would be a great time for him to reconnect with Kat. He highly doubted it. Kat's mother despised him until the day she died. He was the last person she would want at her funeral. He could bet on it. Still, he felt somewhat responsible for Kat and her mother feuding all those years ago. How would Kat react when she saw him at the funeral?

If her mother hadn't caught him in bed with her teenage daughter, Kat may have stayed in Side Lake. It was mainly his fault they were estranged when she died. Although it was Kat's mother's fault, he and Kat never built a life together. They never got to say goodbye or see if their relationship would work out. She was too busy trying to keep them as far apart as possible.

JENNIFER WALTERS

"I've had something eating me up for over a decade and I really need to tell someone."

Kevin buckled up. "Nice to see you too, man. But seriously, let's hear it."

"If you tell your woman, it could be a problem."

"It's not my secret to tell."

"I was hoping you would say that, but it's pretty big."

Kevin exhaled. "Sounds like you need to get it out."

"You have no idea."

"Shoot."

Kevin had no clue he was about to tell him a huge secret, although he may already know the secret. He needed to find out if Kevin knew, and the only way to know was to spit it out and see if Kevin knew after all.

"You know, the day Kat left the lake all those years ago."

"Yeah. I remember Lyndsey telling me not to come over because she was having a girl's day with Kat, and then suddenly she told me Kat's mom came to get her and she wasn't coming back. What about it?"

"Well, did Lyndsey tell you she had to deliver a letter to me from Kat?"

"Yeah," Kevin said. "She had a hard time because Kat told her not to open it and not reading it was killing her because Kat made such a big deal about her privacy and trust. What was in that letter, anyway?"

"Are you sure Lyndsey didn't read the letter?"

"She said she didn't, and I believe her."

He squinted at Kevin, trying to decide whether or not he believed him.

"I'm being real. If she did, she didn't tell me," Kevin said, snapping. "Why? What is this all about, Ethan?"

He took a deep breath. "Kat was pregnant."

"What?!"

Kevin gasped, and his face reflected his shock. He looked around and then whispered, "She was pregnant?"

"She said she was pregnant, and that was why her mother took a while to kick her out. She was going to the Cities to live with her aunt and have the baby, and she was signing her rights away. The same was asked of me in that letter."

"What the hell? How did I not know about this?"

"Obviously, it was a secret. I'm not even sure Lyndsey knows."

"You got that right!" Kevin said, looking away. "Why would you tell me this?"

"Because I needed to tell someone."

"What ended up happening?" Kevin asked.

"I'm not sure. I haven't talked to Kat since. I had to meet at an attorney's office with my parents to sign off, and the attorney said they found a home for our child. That's all I know. I heard nothing after that."

"You didn't try to get ahold of Kat since she was having your child?"

"Of course, I did. I wrote her letters. I tried to find her, but Lyndsey didn't even know where she lived at that time. Kat made her swear not to give me her number because her mother was looking at her phone records to make sure we weren't in contact. She thought I was Satan. I was sworn to secrecy. I gave her some space and now..."

"And now?"

"And now I realize I should have tried harder," Ethan said, looking down at his hands.

"You think?"

"I was young, okay? A part of me was relieved I wouldn't have to take responsibility for a child when I found out. It's horrible, I know. It sounds worse when I say it out loud. But it's her fault, too. She never tried to find me when she knew where I lived and where I spent my summers back then."

Kevin looked angry, and Ethan regretted telling him. He didn't want this to get back to Lyndsey before Kat had a chance to tell her.

"I can't believe you went through all this and never told me. How did your parents react?"

"They supported my decision," Ethan said. "It wasn't an easy decision to make."

"I hate Lyndsey doesn't know about this. It would kill her. And if Kat never told her, it could ruin their friendship.

"That's why you're going to keep it a secret," Ethan said, with a warning in his voice.

"Great, now I'll be on Lyndsey's shit list, too. Thanks." Kevin threw up his hands.

Maybe he should have talked to Kat before telling Kevin.

"I think Lyndsey knows, and she was sworn to secrecy." He in no way believed this to be true, but he could not let the guilt of this secret destroy his friend.

He nodded, staring out the window. "I'll believe that's true because otherwise, this could put a huge wedge in between Lyndsey and me, or Kat and Lyndsey."

"I won't let it."

"It may be out of your control."

Five

Kat

Kat's aunt, Lyndsey, and most of Side Lake surrounded her mother's lifeless body in the casket. The funeral home did an amazing job at making her mother look beautiful and peaceful, like she was just taking a nap.

For the first time in a long time, a few of the good memories came back. Her mother teaching her to bake Christmas cookies, building sandcastles together down by the beach, the summers they went jet skiing, and when her mother surprised her with a water trampoline.

All the kids in Side Lake wanted to play at her house growing up because of the waterslide and trampoline out by her dock. Her mother was well known for being an excellent hostess and making all the neighborhood kids' snacks. She was so different when Kat was little. Guarded and sad, but like she was still trying to be a good mother.

By the time Kat was a teenager, her mother became

uptight and strict. A smile never crossed her face, and she never let any of Kat's friends come over. Kat had a hard time figuring out what made her change so much.

She shook away the memories. Her mother had not spoken to her in years. Now, even after she was gone, Kat struggled to forgive her for everything she did. Not thinking about her was easier.

Now she was at her mother's funeral. She would have to hug the people who came, hear their condolences, and she probably would not shed another tear. Wakes always bothered her. The family left behind had to endure a revolving door of sadness and hugs. For her, having to talk to people when she just wanted to be alone was a special kind of torture.

Her aunt led a few of the kids into the back room to play because she could tell they were getting restless.

Lyndsey put her arm around her back. "How are you doing?"

Kat smiled. "I'm okay. A little nervous to see everyone after all these years. Coming back was hard enough."

"I know it was, and I'm proud of you. I'm also selfishly happy to have you here again. You just let me know what you need, okay? This is just a way for everyone to say goodbye to your mom."

She took Lyndsey's hand and followed her aunt next to the casket. The picture boards were mainly of her mother's younger years. Her aunt had dug through albums to find pictures to put on the board, and she could not find many recent pictures.

She hated having to face her childhood again by looking at the pictures and everything about her old life she tried to forget. The life she decided to put behind her years ago. It hurt too much to think about everything she went through, and she needed all her energy to make it through this day.

More people started coming in. Erma, who worked at the post office at the lake when she was young, was one of the first in line to greet her. She made eye contact with Kat and opened her arms wide to give her a big hug.

"Look at you, all grown up."

She did her best to smile, but nervous laughter followed.

"You look beautiful. If you need any help at the house, please call me. So great to see you again. I hope you stick around town for a while. We miss you."

She shook off her nerves and leaned over to Lyndsey. "Does she still work at the post office?"

"Yes, she does. I don't know what the town will do the day she retires. She's the sweetest lady and a stickler for detail. Not a letter gets put in the wrong mailbox."

Kat nodded. After all this time, things had not changed that much.

Gabby and Matt Fredrickson came in and gave her a hug. "I'm so sorry you're going through this. If you need anything, please call," Gabby said.

"Thank you for coming," Kat said. She surprised herself because she meant it. The Fredrickson's had their own hard losses as children. They understood what it felt like to lose a parent.

They made more small talk and promises of getting together.

Some people told her they were sorry for her loss and others told her how great it was to see her. Every person at the funeral knew of the struggles between her and her mother. It was never a secret. Although she was pretty sure few knew about her young pregnancy. The pregnancy embarrassed and ashamed her mother because it made her look like a less than perfect mother for allowing it to happen. Her mother's status always meant more than her own daughter, and she would never forgive her for that.

The line finally shortened, and she relaxed a bit.

A magnetic force drew her toward the door as he walked in. He was even more handsome than he had been when they were younger. His bright blue button-up shirt made his eyes stand out, and his striped tie was perfectly matched. He stared at her with his hands in his pockets and flashed her a nervous smile.

Her face grew warm, and she could not keep her eyes off him as she hugged the next person in line.

At first, she worried he and Kevin were going to sit down without talking to her, but they surprised her by getting back up and coming to stand in line.

Finally, they were next in line. She hugged Kevin.

"How are you doing?"

"I'm doing," she said. "Thanks for coming and for letting me borrow Lyndsey." She tried to focus on Kevin and not on who was standing next to him. She scrunched her hands in fists to hide the way they shook.

Kevin moved on to hug Lyndsey and left her face-to-face with Ethan.

What should she say? Her face grew warm up again, and she tried to force out his name, but her voice was so shaky it came out as "Ea-ah."

He smiled and pulled her in for a hug. He seemed genuine but also unsure of how to act.

"I know I'm not your favorite person but let's call a truce today, okay?" he whispered in her ear. "I'm so sorry for everything you are going through. Instead of being mad at me for showing up after all these years, imagine what your mom would say if she knew I came to her funeral."

She smiled. "She'd be rolling over in her grave. I'm glad you came, but I'm still mad at you."

She could tell he was holding back what he wanted to say, and she respected that. Later she would tell him how she really felt. Right now, she needed to get through her mother's funeral.

"This reunion really put the fun in funeral," Kevin whispered, too loudly.

Kat glared at him, and Lyndsey elbowed him in the stomach. He groaned and rubbed his stomach at the point of contact.

Ethan leaned in and hugged her again as if he hadn't heard Kevin's inappropriate comment.

He smelled so good. How did a man smell that good? It wasn't cologne or body spray, it was just Ethan. So amazing and sensual. For one moment, he made her forget where she was and all that happened. He made her forget how much she hated him for what he did or didn't do.

Her aunt stepped in front of the first row of pews. "The pastor is ready to start."

"Okay," Kat said, not letting her eyes follow Ethan to the back of the room. He was a handsome distraction, which was exactly what she needed right now to lessen the pain.

Lyndsey sat in the open chair next to Kat and leaned over to whisper in her ear. "Is it just me, or is it hot in here?"

"I don't know what you mean," she said, trying to hide the way she really felt.

"Sure you don't. I think everyone in this room felt the sexual tension between the two of you."

Kat rolled her eyes and leaned toward her friend. "I don't know what you think you saw, but I still hate him."

"Sure you do."

"He's just as cocky as he was when we were teenagers."

The pastor began to speak. Good, she would not need to defend herself to Lyndsey anymore. She hated how Lyndsey could read her.

She tuned out the pastor's words. All she could think about was getting out of there as fast as she could when the funeral was over. She would say something at the luncheon, but not here.

Once the pastor gave her a nod of respect, signaling he was done, she grabbed Lyndsey's hand and pulled her out of the church before someone could stop her and hug her or give her a look of pity.

The warm, muggy air greeted them as they walked out the door and to her car. She started her car and backed up, her head turned around to look out the back window. She pulled forward and saw Ethan exit the funeral home in her rear-view mirror, watching her as she pulled away.

"Sorry, I needed to get out of there," she told Lyndsey. "It was overwhelming. I'll be drinking a lot at the luncheon."

"No judgement here. I get it. You okay? You know, I was just giving you crap about Ethan."

"I know. Is it horrible that the whole time the pastor was talking about my mom, I kept thinking about all the things I wanted to say to Ethan. Like what a jerk he is?" He had to come back into her life after all these years with his perfect hair, a tight shirt that showed he obviously took care of himself, and that butt.

"And how good he looked?" Lyndsey said, reading her mind.

Kat laughed and laughed and soon Lyndsey was laughing, too.

"I may hate him, but he was a great distraction," she said.

"I'm sorry, but even I kept thinking about the interaction between the two of you. I did not know you had such a connection after all this time. You two were just teenagers the last time you saw each other?"

"Yes, a long time ago. I hope he doesn't think I'm into him

like that anymore because I'm not. I had a moment of weakness, that's all. No one else seemed to notice."

"Are you kidding me? I think the pastor could feel the heat."

"You're not helping, Lyndsey," Kat said as she shook her head. "I have a boyfriend and Ethan Iverson is the last person I would ever have a crush on. He broke my heart once. Never again."

"You're still dating Andy? I'm surprised he wasn't here for the funeral."

"He, ah… couldn't get off work," she lied.

The truth was, she did not want Andy to come to Side Lake.

"But Ethan is here, and he's hot and some obvious heat is going on. The way I see it, there's no harm in a little flirting," Lyndsey said sweetly. "Maybe this is your mom's way of apologizing for all the terrible things she did to you."

"The only heat you'll see from now on is my anger toward him. I'm going to give him a piece of my mind."

Lyndsey rolled down her window halfway. "Sure you are."

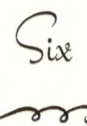

Six

Ethan

Ethan dropped Kevin off at Lyndsey's house to change, then he headed to Bimbo's restaurant for a cold beer before meeting up with Kat. He needed to take the edge off and calm his nerves before he saw her again. But all he thought about was the way she felt in his arms before she dismissed him, and Kevin made that stupid comment. Despite making it clear she was still angry, she seemed glad he was there, maybe? And she had been checking him out when he walked in. He checked her out, too. She was even more beautiful now than when they were teens. An electricity sparked between them. Still, he was angry at her for cutting him out of her life without having the guts to say goodbye in person.

She hid behind a stupid letter he read over and over for years. Each time it broke his heart all over again. But then again, she thanked him for being there. Maybe that was her olive branch.

He was on his second beer when she walked in the door with Kevin and Brad. Here we go. He got off his bar stool and leaned over the bar to get the bartender's attention.

The bartender made eye contact and walked his way. "Bring me a Tequila Sunrise." He tipped the bartender a twenty and followed Kat and the rest of the group into the back room.

A buffet of various kinds of pizza lined one wall. Bimbo's was well known for their pizza and wings. Comfort food was exactly what Ethan needed after this day. He had to keep his hands and his mouth busy. He was there to support Kat, not hit on her.

Writing came to him naturally. Talking on the spot, not so much.

Kat was sitting at the table. Her long hair glowed as the sun shone through the windows. She was talking to Lyndsey when he touched her shoulder with a cold glass. She turned around quickly.

She laughed and stood up, then crossed her arms with a suspicious look. "Double fisting it, huh?" She looked at the drinks. "I never would have taken you for a fruity drink kind of guy."

"Actually, this one is for you."

She pointed at her chest and then took the drink. "You best not be trying to poison me. You know what? Never mind, today I'll take the chance. I'm pretty sure this day couldn't get any worse." She took a sip, then stared at it with a disgusted look on her face. "What is this? A Sex on the Beach?"

"Tequila Sunrise."

She shrugged and gulped it down. "Not bad."

"I'm glad you liked it."

"If you think this means I'm going to forgive you for everything you did to me, you're wrong."

"Oh, really? Everything I did?" He leaned into her ear and

whispered, "You're so lucky I'm feeling like a gentleman right now or I'd set you straight."

Her mouth widened, and her eyes turned cold. "Is that a threat?"

He did not answer.

She spoke through clenched teeth, "Do you really think I care what you think? You show up at my mother's funeral, flex your muscles around, show off your white teeth and expensive clothes and think all is forgiven? Then you have the balls to say you're mad at me? I don't think so."

He grinned. "What happened to the truce?"

She seemed to think about it. "Get me a Crown and Coke and I promise not to throw pillows at you, Mr. Iverson."

Her comment only made him grin more. She was thinking about that night. That night was probably keeping her mind off everything going on in her world right now and for that, he was glad. Even if she kept dishing out the comments that had his blood boiling. She went from being so angry she did everything but spit in his face, to being flirty and throw reminders his way that she saw him naked.

He came back with her Crown and Coke in a lowball glass and stood behind her as she talked to one of the Side Lake ladies.

As a teenager, she had been this sex goddess. She was beautiful and confident in an inexperienced way. But now, she was naturally gorgeous. Short and sweet, a beautiful figure with curves, and she hardly wore any makeup. Her clothes were elegant and conservative as opposed to her low-cut shirts and short shorts when she was a teenager. Her mouth was even sassier now, but he appreciated it. Encouraged it, really. After their history, he expected nothing less from her.

How did he find himself even more attracted to her than back then? Maybe because she was not trying so hard to impress him.

He rested his face into a more serious expression and put his hand on her shoulder so he could hand her the glass.

"Thank you. You're surprisingly compliant," she whispered. She lifted her smile and batted her eyelashes at him.

"Don't get used to it," he whispered back into her ear.

She bit her lip. "We'll see about that."

"Katrina, dear, Mrs. Finney is looking for you," her aunt said with a gentle nudge and continued to walk away.

Ethan saw her expression turn sad.

"Is it getting any better?"

"Is what getting better?" She paused and frowned and stared at him.

He hung his head. "This," he said, as he waved his glass around him to point out the room full of people that surrounded them.

She looked around and leaned in close to him. His body reacted with goosebumps to her lips touching his ear. "Everyone knows I never got along with my mom. It's just so weird. Half the people don't say anything about her to me, and the other half are trying to tell me how sorry they were, as if it was too bad I never got to know her better. I feel so fake. Like a fraud and the worst part is I know they aren't trying to be mean. I know they aren't sure what to say." She held her glass above eye level. "This is going to help a lot more than that sissy drink you gave me. Shows you don't know me at all. Now, if you'll excuse me—"

Ethan shook his head and clinked his drink against her glass before she could step away. "I'm glad I could help."

Kevin's mother walked up and put her arms around Kat's shoulders. "It's so great to see you back here, dear. How are you doing?"

"I'm okay. So excited for this to be over, I guess."

"I didn't know your mom well, but she was a heck of a bridge player. Did she ever teach you?"

Ethan stepped in to save her. "I didn't know you played bridge, Mrs. Finney. Did Troy and Kevin play too?"

For the next hour, Kat tried to entertain her guests with a fake smile as she listened to their stories about her mother and pretended to care. But the effort was getting to her. Ethan saw it in her beautiful blue eyes. They were glazed over and sad. From the puffiness of her eyelids, her mother's death had an enormous effect on her she would never admit to.

After three drinks, he stopped drinking so he could stay somewhat sober for Kat. He wanted to be there for her in case she needed him, and he could not do that if his thinking was cloudy.

"Everyone, can I have your attention?" Kat said, hitting her glass with a fork to get their attention.

The room got quiet.

"As many of you know, my mother and I weren't on the best of terms. Hell, she threw me out when I was a teenager because I didn't fit into her perfect little lifestyle." She used air quotes, her words a bit slurred.

He debated whether he should step in and stop her from drinking anymore. Would she regret whatever she was going to say? If only he knew what was going to come out of her mouth.

"But she loved you, dear. She truly did," Kevin's mother said, squeezing her shoulder.

Kat pulled away. "She didn't love me. She abandoned me. Anyway, I just want to let you all know she may have fooled all of you, but she was evil to me, her own flesh and blood. She sent me away when I needed her the most, and yet here I am. Back in the one place I promised myself I would never return to. The place is full of terrible memories and anger."

Ethan stepped forward and tried to lightly guide her away. She shrugged him off.

"It's my turn to talk, Ethan. My turn." She looked back at the people. "She played you all, played every one of you because she cared so much about keeping up with her reputation and not looking bad. She didn't love me, and she didn't love you. She was just pure evil and played you all for a fool."

Lyndsey leaned forward and whispered something in Kat's ear.

"Fine, fine," Kat said, she almost fell over. "Enjoy the food and grieve everyone. I hope you have some good memories because I sure as hell don't. Mic drop," she said dramatically.

She dropped her drink on the ground, alcohol splashed up her legs, but the glass somehow remained in one piece on the floor.

Lyndsey whispered to him, "Will you please drive her home? I'll take care of everything here. I know this isn't your problem, but you're the only sober person here that I can ask. The only person who probably agrees with every word she just said."

"Not a problem," Ethan said. "Come on, Kat." He grabbed her arm gently to lead her toward the door.

She resisted at first and then gave in. "Fine, but I still hate you."

Kat walked beside him a couple of steps, then stopped and mumbled under her breath.

The guests whispered out of genuine concern for Kat. Lyndsey took over and addressed them, which drew their attention away from Kat. Ethan picked Kat up when no one was looking, and carried her to his truck.

He got her into his car and shut the door, then climbed in behind the wheel.

"You know what, Ethan Iverson?" She said when she looked over at him.

He looked back at her and hoped she would not say something she was going to regret tomorrow.

"What's that?"

"I may despise you, but I have never stopped thinking about you."

She fell forward, and he caught her. Her seatbelt kept her from hitting the dashboard. Her head crashed to her chest, and she snored loudly.

He drove her home with only the slight sound of the radio playing on low, and her soft snores. He kept glancing at her. So many emotions coursed through him when he was around Kat. None of this was easy for her. She'd been through so much. He bought her the drinks and told her it would help. Drinking only made everything worse.

As he pulled up to her garage, he put the truck in park and ran around to open her door. She was still out cold. He unbuckled her seatbelt and slid her body toward him. He tried to move her without waking her, but her eyes opened.

She tapped his nose with her pointer finger. "It wasn't a dream. Ethan Iverson is here, and he is being such a gentleman."

He caught her finger and squeezed it. "Can you walk, or would you like me to carry you?"

As soon as she stepped out of the truck, her knees buckled beneath her. She caught herself on the door and started laughing and fell to her knees in her beautiful dress. Ethan helped her up.

She brushed him off a couple times, then let him help her once she realized her legs were rubbery, and she could not stand on her own.

"I'm wasted. I never get wasted. I hate losing control."

"Let's get you inside," he said. He guided her by her arm to the side door, which was wide open. He picked her up again and carried her inside.

"Which way?"

"That way," she said, pointing at the wall.

Not very helpful.

He found the first open room upstairs and gently laid her on the bed and removed her shoes. He picked up a blue blanket lying at the end of the bed and draped it over her.

Kat grabbed onto the front of his shirt, fisted it, and pulled him toward her.

"Don't go," she pleaded.

This was a bad idea, but she looked so scared.

"Lie with me. Please, Ethan."

Her big blue eyes silently begged him. How could he say no?

He lay down next to her. How did he get himself into this position? She was drunk and did not know what she was saying, but her eyes showed fear and he could not bring himself to leave her there by herself.

She slid over and spooned with him, then grabbed his arms and wrapped them around her. This was trouble. He would sneak out before she woke up in the morning because she would not be okay with this when she woke up. He did not want to upset her. She had been through enough.

Would she be angry tomorrow when she realized what she said to all those people at the luncheon? That she made him lie with her? Yep. She would be so angry and it would somehow end up his fault. His one hope was she was too drunk to remember anything.

He wanted to ask her so many questions about their past, but would there ever be an opportunity when all she wanted to do was push him away?

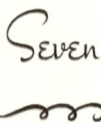

Seven

Kat

She opened her eyes to large green trees waving on the other side of three huge floor-to-ceiling windows. Her body became weak and her heart beat in overdrive. This was her mother's room.

She could not remember how old she was the last time she crawled into bed with her mother, but she would never forget that night. She was maybe five or six sleeping in her bedroom when a storm began. Lightning flashed outside her window and she sat up in bed. Her bedroom light flashed, and the thunder and lightning struck at almost the same time so the storm was close. She was afraid the lightning would come through her window and start a fire.

She made a mad dash to her mother's room.

"Mama," she had said. "Mama, I'm scared."

"Oh, sweetheart." Her mother picked her up and held her

close to her chest as she made her way to the bed. They crawled under the covers and her mother ran her fingers through her hair to calm her.

The memory of that night was one of the happiest memories of her mother. So happy, she sometimes wondered if she had dreamt it. Not long after that, her mother started locking her doors and stayed up most nights boozing. There was always a drink in her hand and a wobble in her step once the clock struck six. It was as if there was a time that justified getting wasted just so she wouldn't have to face reality.

She sat up in bed and rubbed her eyes. She was all alone in her mother's room. Well, that was a relief. She got out of bed and sighed in relief that she was fully clothed.

She was so glad yesterday was over. If only she knew how she got home from Bimbo's and why she crawled into her mother's bed. She was drunk. That must be the reason. She just hoped she was not dumb enough to drink and drive home.

After she made the bed, she went downstairs to put on some coffee and stared at the bookshelf and ladder. She was in disbelief that her mother actually got the ladder she had begged for when she was ten. She grabbed onto the shelf at eye level and pulled on it to test its sturdiness, jiggled the ladder and pulled on it to test the stability.

"Well, here goes nothing."

With both feet on the ladder, she grabbed onto the bookshelf. The force of her push sent the ladder and her flying across the bookshelf so fast she struggled to hold on.

It stopped abruptly, and she flew off the ladder and hit the wall next to the bookshelf. She landed on the floor on her back, the wind knocked out of her. Laughter bubbled up as she stared up at the ceiling. The longer she lay there, the harder she laughed at what she just did.

"Kat?"

She kept laughing.

"What are you doing?"

Lyndsey stood over her, shaking her head. She looked up at the ladder, then down at Kat. "Don't tell me you tested out the ladder to see how fast it could go without me?"

Now they were both laughing until Kat noticed she was the only one still laughing. Lyndsey's expression was filled with concern.

Kat wiped her face. Her fingers were wet, but not with blood. Tears were streaming down her face and she didn't even notice. She was no longer laughing, but crying. Crying was becoming a regular occurrence. Her mother had turned her weak.

"Are you okay?"

Kat stared into her friend's eyes. "Yeah, I'm not sure why I'm crying. Can you help me up?"

Lyndsey held out her hand, and Kat jumped to her feet.

"I think I had a little too much to drink last night."

"As you should. It was your mother's funeral. Who would want to be sober for that?"

She had a point.

"I was kind of hoping to find Ethan here with you this morning."

She turned her head so fast she almost pulled a muscle in her neck. "Why would you say that?"

"Because he gave you a ride home."

Uh-oh, that was how she got home. She let herself get so drunk she blacked out. She slapped her forehead.

"Ouch," Lyndsey said with a curious look. "That sounded like it hurt."

"Now it makes sense. I thought it was strange that I woke

up in my mom's bed this morning with no idea how I got there. Ethan must have put me to bed in the first room he found."

"That was sweet of him," she said, staring at Kat.

"I guess." She paused. She wasn't comfortable with him seeing her like that.

Lyndsey sat down on the couch. "Exactly. The two of you were so in love when we were kids. And here you are again and he's back, too. What are the odds?"

Her friend was trying to start something that was no longer there. She and Ethan had not talked for years. Nothing was between them anymore. Ethan had not waited around all these years for her, that's for certain.

"I'll see if there's some tea in the kitchen. Want some?"

"Sure. I'll grab another box to sort through. Enough fun and games for this girl," Kat said.

She opened another box with her name on it. The furry purple unicorn was on top. She smiled as she pulled it out and held it close. Her favorite stuffed animal when she was a child. She squeezed it and memories of the happy times from her childhood with her unicorn returned. But the memory of her mother telling her she was too old for the unicorn came back to her and she set it down. She found a scrapbook with her name on the front and some pictures that she drew as a child.

Time for the next box. She walked up the stairs with the box and tripped. The box fell on its side and opened.

Lyndsey peeked around the stairs. "You okay?"

"I'm fine," she said, her voice interrupted by the whistling of the teapot. "Go ahead and make the tea. I'll clean up this mess."

"Okay."

She stuffed the jackets back in the box and then a book slipped through and went tumbling down the stairs. She picked up the box and set it down next to the book at the bottom of the stairs.

She opened up the book, unsure of what it was. The book was filled with handwriting and at the bottom of the page a signature, xx Krystal. This was her mother's handwriting. She flipped back to the first page.

My doctor told me I need to start journaling, so here I am journaling. I'm not really sure how to journal. As a child, I never had a diary or even liked to write in a notebook like everyone else. I was told this is supposed to be freeing. Ha! I will never be free. I've pushed everyone away in my life. I guess it is time to deal with that now, or so I'm told. I get this anger that starts deep in my core and shoots up like fire, making me unable to see clearly. I rage and I can't come back down to reality. Some nights I wake up and I'm drenched in my sweat. It's quite disgusting, really.

When I got the news that I was sick, I felt nothing but relief. It's really weird. I would like to think I was normal before that day on my sixteenth birthday when my mom found out I was pregnant. I can't put my finger on the moment I broke, but I know it was that day. I don't deny thinking about having an abortion, but my mother quickly told me it was not an option. After that, I was no longer a part of my body, disconnected from everything. I didn't want to be a mother and I never even thought about having a child someday. It was my mother's plan, and I couldn't argue with her. My sweet sixteen was the day I stopped smiling and the day I could no longer see past the darkness.

I wanted to love my baby in my belly. I really did, but I no longer had feelings or emotions. I was numb. Six months later, my mother sat beside me, holding my hand as Kat was born. I didn't name her. I couldn't. My mom named her. I was not ready to be a mom. Here I was holding this beautiful baby and inside I was dead. What is wrong with me?

xx Krystal

She stuffed the notebook under the pillow on her bed. This was more than she had ever known about why her mother was the way she was. It showed just the smallest amount of vulnerability, and for the first time, Kat actually felt like maybe her mother was not as emotionless as she thought.

Lyndsey was in the kitchen pouring the hot water and putting tea bags into travel cups.

"I'm on my way to clean the cabins now. You need to take a break and come with me."

It was not a question. "I don't know, I…"

"We can go through more things later. You need to take a break. Besides, it's a beautiful day," she said, pointing out the window.

The sun was shining in the blue sky and not a cloud was in sight.

"You can go to the beach and stare out at the water, maybe take a dip in the lake. It will be a nice break," Lyndsey said.

Kat ran her fingers through her hair. She kept thinking about the journal, but relaxing by the lake would be good.

She nodded, and Lyndsey's face lit up. "We'll have so much fun! I promise." She headed for her car, but turned around. "Oh, and don't forget your suit."

Kat followed Lindsey through all six cabins at Pine Beach as she cleaned. She tried many times to help, but all Lyndsey would let her do was sweep the floor.

"I didn't bring you here to work. I brought you here to keep me company. It's so great to have you back here."

"I really missed this place, but..." She could not find the words.

"But it gives you some anxiety? You aren't sure you want to be back here? It's weird?"

Kat stood up and laughed. "Exactly. You read my mind. It's just so weird. I expect her to come through the door and start getting on my case about something. I'm glad she isn't here, yet I didn't want her to die. It makes no sense really."

"Oh, I understand. You went through hell with her. Although I've always wondered what actually happened."

Kat sat up straight. "What do you mean?"

"I've never pushed, but I always knew you weren't telling me something.." Lyndsey touched Kat's shoulder. "I hope one day you'll trust me enough to tell me."

She always knew Lyndsey had her suspicions about why she moved away. Sure, Lyndsey knew how terrible her mother was, but she also knew there was a secret. Lyndsey respected her silence, but it was time to tell her the truth.

"The truth is—"

The door flew open before she could finish her sentence. In walked Ethan with no shirt, earbuds, and a little strut to his step as he bent over to take off his shoes. He hadn't seen them yet.

He dropped to the floor and began doing one armed push-ups, his mind obviously preoccupied. He grunted, and the sweat glowed on his back. His shoulders and back flexed, showing off his chiseled muscles and his well-defined calves. She looked away in case he caught her staring at him.

Her face grew warm when Lyndsey's eyes caught hers. Busted. Lyndsey would give her so much crap, but she could not take her eyes off him. The bulge in every movement.

Lyndsey raised her eyebrows and covered her mouth as she watched Kat and then Ethan.

After what felt like hours, he stood back up and stopped mid-step, almost tripping on his own feet. He yanked an ear bud out.

"Kat? What are you doing here?"

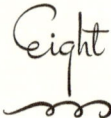

Eight

Ethan

Was she really in his cabin? Why? Here he was, standing in front of the woman he thought about every day. The way she snuggled into him in her bed last night, begging him to stay. He stared into her eyes as he thought about the way her skin felt next to his last night. He looked away. She was far from sober and probably had no recollection of it.

Sweat dripped down his forehead and chest. This was not the way he wanted to run into her. A thought occurred. Was she here to yell at him for last night? Maybe she remembered, and she was angry.

Kat gasped. "I'm so sorry. I didn't know—didn't realize this was..."

She seemed to be at a loss for words. Why? Did he make her uncomfortable? Was she embarrassed about the way she acted last night?

She looked past him and took two steps toward the door. "I should go," she said before bolting out the door.

He wanted to stop her, but his body was paralyzed. The door closed, and he turned to Lyndsey for some explanation of what just happened. Did he do something wrong?

"Well then. That wasn't awkward at all," Lyndsey said with a nervous laugh. "I'm sorry about that. I think she has a lot on her mind."

"Was it me? Did I do something to make her feel that way?"

"No. I mean, look at you. Your muscles are all ripped and bulging, and you're half naked. I don't think she knew how to react. I'm sure last night didn't help either."

He threw up his arms in surrender. "Last night? Nothing happened, I promise. I brought her home just like you asked."

"I know that, and she knows that, but she woke up in her mother's bed and didn't know how she got there."

"Her mother's bed?" Oh no. How was he so stupid that he never realized it was her mother's bedroom? That must have devastated her when she woke up.

"I think I'd be just as embarrassed if I were in her shoes." Lyndsey shook her head and grinned. "She was drunk, and you had to carry her home. She's convinced she hates you, you know."

He dug his fingers into his eyes. "I can't believe I'm such an idiot."

She patted him on his back. "Don't be so hard on yourself, it's sweet. She just lost her mom, and she doesn't know how to feel about it. Give her some time."

"Is she staying?" He hoped he hadn't scared her away. She knew how to get under his skin, but he enjoyed the way they went back and forth. He hoped trying to be helpful last night hadn't ruined everything.

"I don't think Kat knows the answer to that right now.

What I know is she has a lot of stuff to go through and a lot of decisions to make, so I'd guess she'll be here for a while."

"She hates me, doesn't she?"

Lyndsey frowned. "No, but she doesn't know what to think right now. She's been gone a long time, and she has so many mixed emotions. It's as if her childhood just came crashing down on her at full force and smacked her upside the head."

Ethan shook his head and smiled.

"Sorry. Maybe that wasn't the best analogy, but you know what I mean," she said. "I'm going now. I'm really sorry about that."

"No, Lyndsey, don't be. You were doing your job by cleaning. I get it. You didn't know I was coming back so soon."

She gave him a grateful nod and picked up her cleaning basket and left.

He stood in the doorway, all alone, and did the only thing he knew to calm his mind. He walked over to his desk, opened his computer, and wrote.

He kept writing until close to dinnertime. His legs were cramped, his bladder full, and he had a bit of cotton mouth from dehydration.

Every time he saw Kat, the ideas came rushing to him. This town had him writing faster and better than he had in years. He checked his word count for today. Six thousand words. He sat back down and relaxed as his fingers and mind worked together to create more magic.

By seven, he was ready for a break. Everything hurt, and he needed to stretch and exercise. He pulled on the string that opened the blinds and spotted the kayaks. Just what he needed. He had at least two hours before the sun went down.

He made his way down to the docks. Two young boys were playing catch with a football, and a couple holding hands sat on the porch swing that looked out over the water. Loons floated undisturbed on the calm lake. Everyone must be in for the night.

Two kayaks, one blue, the other red, lay on the shore. Both had paddles next to them.

"It's a nice night for kayaking," someone said behind him.

He turned around to find a teenage girl walking toward him.

"It sure is," he said. "Do you know which ones the resort owns?"

"You can take whichever one you want. They're all free game. Although, I was planning on taking the blue one, if you don't mind. I'm Emma, by the way. My parents own the resort."

He remembered her parents having her and her brother. She was just a couple of years old the last time he spent his summer here.

There was something about her eyes that seemed familiar. He could have sworn he met her before. She had to be in her mid-teens.

"Nice to meet you. Can I give you a hand?" He picked up the blue kayak and put it in the water, holding it while she got in.

"Thank you. You're more than welcome to join me if you like."

"That would be great."

He flipped over the other kayak and put it in the water. She was already far out when he started paddling.

Emma looked back at him and yelled out, "Let's head to the channel. Have you been out on the chain before?"

"Yes. I spent many summers at your resort growing up with my family. We used to be permanent campers here."

"Oh, really? That must have been before I was born. Was that back when they used to have a dance floor?"

"Hey, I'm not that old," he said with a laugh. "That was

long before my time. I actually didn't start coming out here until I was in seventh grade. I heard about it, though."

They rowed past cabins on their way to the channel. The loons hardly moved as they maneuvered around them. A bald eagle flew over their heads and circled above them before making its way to the same nest he spotted the other day.

They rounded the corner, and a bridge, different from the one he remembered, came into view. "Did they rebuild the bridge? It looks nice."

"Yeah, a couple of years ago. Much better than the old one."

"It's beautiful," he said, trying to remember what the old one looked like.

"It gets shallow for some boats under this bridge." She stood her paddle in the water until it touched the ground. It had to be only three feet deep under them. "The ones with fins have to center their boats perfectly when they go under. Some rocks from the old bridge are still under the water, so they have to be careful."

He and Emma were in sync as they rowed at a steady pace.

Ethan swatted at a horse fly before returning to paddling. "Do you like living in Side Lake?"

"Yeah. A lot of my friends camp with their families in the summer, but in the winter it gets quiet around here. Some of my friends live around the lake, too. It's pretty much just us at the resort in the winter and people that come and go renting out the cabins at our resort for snowmobiling and cross-country skiing."

"So, it's just you and your brother Dave, right? No other siblings?"

She was paddling at his side now. "Nope, just us."

"You both help your parents with the upkeep at the resort, then?"

"Yeah. I also work at Bimbo's making pizzas or bartending

and waitressing. I go wherever I'm needed. It's nice to have a little break, but my parents pay me for the time I put in. I've been doing it since I was young."

He was impressed with her motivation. "Owning a resort is a lot of work."

"Yeah, they hire cleaners because it's too much for just us. My parents are getting older now. It's a lot for them."

"I can imagine."

They stayed to the side of the channel to make room in case a boat came along. Lily pads lined the outside of the channel, and frogs jumped along the shoreline.

He swatted at bugs flying around them, disturbed by the movement.

"It's getting late. Want to turn back?" Emma turned the kayak around before he answered.

The channel took ten minutes to get through idling in a boat, so he expected it would take them a long time to reach the next lake in a kayak. Although he was enjoying himself, he needed to get more writing done. The lake was inspiring his creativity.

"You read my mind. It'll be dark soon."

"So, Ethan, do you still have friends who live around the lake?"

"Yeah. Well, we've lost touch over the years, but I grew up best friends with Brad and Lyndsey Jones, Kevin Finney, and my friend Kat, who moved away a long time ago. Do you know them? I know Lyndsey works at your resort, so you must know her."

"I don't know her really well, but she seems nice. I don't know the others. How come you lost touch?"

"Long story," he said, in a quiet voice.

"Did you have a girlfriend here?"

"Yes, I briefly dated Kat one summer. She left Side Lake

many years ago and just recently came back because her mother passed away."

"Oh, her mother must be Krystal. I know her, knew her." She corrected herself. "She lived on Turtle Creek Road. So sad about her sudden death. Your friend must be devastated."

"Yeah." Kat's mother put her through hell and he struggled not to say it under his breath.

"Wait, Kevin Finney doesn't happen to be Officer Finney?"

"Yep. You know him then?"

"He's friends of my parents. Maddy and Brad are too." She sighed. "They had an enormous loss not too long ago. So sad."

"Yeah, I heard that. So terrible." He couldn't believe it took this long for him to hear what happened to Brad. "I don't know Maddy. I'm guessing she didn't grow up in Side Lake."

"No, I don't think she did." A few seconds went by. "Mind if I ask what made you come back after all this time?"

"I'm a writer and I wanted some new inspiration. I love Side Lake."

"Me too."

She was the first one to get out of her kayak on shore. He stood up, and the kayak tipped with him. He lost his balance and fell into the water, splashing Emma and drenching himself.

Emma laughed so hard she was down on her knees, trying to catch her breath.

"Oh, you think it's funny when an old man falls into the water, huh?"

She continued laughing and pointing at him.

"It's all fun and games until someone breaks a hip."

He pulled his kayak out of the water and lined it up in the

grass next to hers. Emma finally caught her breath, still looking at him and laughing.

"Well, it was great meeting you, Ethan. Thank you for that. I needed a good laugh."

"Anytime. I'm glad you can laugh at my expense. Thank you for being my tour guide and keeping this old man company."

"Anytime."

Nine

Kat

She was acting like a child, running out like that. What was wrong with her? She could see the hurt in his eyes at the way she acted in there. He made sure she got home safely and tucked her into her mother's bed. How could she run away from him? How embarrassing. He must think she was a mess.

They were a summer fling many years ago, that's all. So why did she feel so attracted to him now? Watching those muscles bulge as he did push-ups like he was a marine enthralled her. But she had a boyfriend. What was she thinking? They had a childhood fling, even if he looked like a model now. He was not good for her, nor was she good for him. Her past needed to stay in her past. And she hated him for what he did.

She cut him off all those years ago with just a letter. She never thought she would have to face him again. The faster she cleaned out the house so she could leave, the better. Reminders of her past were everywhere she looked.

The anger boiled inside her. Her mother ruined her childhood and here she was, stuck with everything, but no answers.

She grabbed a bin and found a picture of her and her mother. Rage burned through her veins. She threw the picture against the bookcase, then threw decorations out of the bin. The angel her mother gave her for her first Christmas stared back at her.

She screamed, "I hate you." She threw the angel, and it hit a plant. Dirt spilled all over the white carpet. She dropped to the floor and sobbed into the carpet.

"Why were you so difficult and stubborn? I hated you! You were evil and mean and—" She let out a scream of frustration. She sounded like a wounded animal and she laughed even as the tears continued to fall. "You would never forgive me for your perfect white carpet getting ruined, but you aren't here anymore, are you? No, you left me, you stubborn old woman." Now she was talking to herself.

She had to clean up the mess, or the carpet would stain. Yet, she hated everything this house stood for. Her mother lived in this giant house all alone because she pushed everyone away.

She returned everything to the bin. At least the angel had not been harmed during her tantrum. When was the last time she got that angry? She kept her emotions hidden deep within her. She did not show her vulnerability to anyone, but finally feeling something felt good.

She cleaned up the mess, but when she lifted the animated Santa, she realized her mother's journal was wet. Panic sank in as she wiped it off the as best as she could. She wanted to keep reading her mother's words. Not because she cared, no, but because she needed to get closure. She had been fighting her emotions for too long, and she needed to see if the answers were in the book somewhere.

She opened it up. The first couple of pages had a little water stain, but not bad enough that it ruined the words. She could still read it.

She opened the journal to the page where she left off.

Kat cries a lot and some nights I'm unable to sleep, but her cries aren't loud and all she wants is to be held. Sometimes my mom gets to her first and when I come into Kat's bedroom, I can see the judgment in my mother's eyes. She doesn't understand why I am so broken and hurt. I haven't told her the truth yet. I prefer sleeping during the day because I hate the light of day and I'd rather just skip it.

Why can't the sun just hide behind the clouds? The moon is so much nicer. It lets off some light to be seen in the darkness, just the way I prefer. I will go back to high school next week. Everyone is going to stare at me. I just know it. They keep asking me who the father is, but I will never tell. I'm scared to face Dennis. When I started showing at school and rumors started, Dennis asked me if the baby could be his, but I told him no because I could see the panic in his eyes as he waited for my reply. He isn't ready. I'm not ready. The relief in his eyes hurt so much. I wanted to take back my words, but I loved him too much. I told him I cheated on him and he hasn't talked to me since. What is wrong with me? He graduates this year and was accepted by the University of Minnesota. He's going places and I don't want him to quit it all for me. Maybe someday I can tell him the truth, but not today. Today I cry alone.

. . .

My mom never asked me whose baby she is. She knew it was Dennis. We'd been together 2 years. Not anymore. He threw me away when all I did was love him. I worry I blame Kat for him leaving me. I'm pretty sure that is why I just can't be a good mom. I was a straight-A student and now I don't care about school at all. I don't want to go back. My mom said she would help me raise Kat, and she is. I've stepped away and worry she will resent me some day. My mom told me I need to go back to being in volleyball and be a teenager, but she doesn't see that I can't and I'm not. I don't fit in anymore. I'm a statistic now. Teen mom. The girl that everyone calls a slut and says I should have used a condom. I want to tell them I did, but they don't hear me over their judging breaths. It's so much easier for them to judge me than to deal with their own messy lives. I am a screw up and I can't even take care of my own baby. I did this all for nothing. I'm trapped in my own skin, and I will never be Krystal again. Not the Krystal I was.

A knock at the door and then a "hello" jerked her out of the journal. Her aunt came walking in.

"What are you doing? Sorting and packing?"

"Aunt Bev, who's Dennis?"

She needed to know that what her mother wrote was true. She had a hard time believing anything her mother ever said or wrote because there were so many lies.

Her aunt froze.

"Who's Dennis?"

"He's um..."

Her aunt fidgeted.

"My mom is gone forever. She isn't going to get mad at you anymore. Who is Dennis and why did she keep him from me?"

"Okay, listen. I know your mom was hard on you and I know you're hurting."

"She did a lot of terrible things to me." Kat looked down at her hands, feeling the pain she felt as a child when her mother hated her and gave up on her. Had her mother ever really loved anyone?

"I know she did, and I'm so sorry about that. Your mom was sick and—"

"Auntie, I need to know who Dennis is. Is he really my father? Is my father not really dead? Did she lie to me about that too? Why did my mom hide this from me?" She felt her cheeks heat up. Why was her aunt so scared to tell her the truth when her mother was no longer around?

"I don't want to hurt you more."

Kat stood up. "I'm an adult. I can take it. Just tell me. I need to know. I need to know why she never wanted me to know."

Her aunt turned away. "Dennis is your father. You're right. And he's alive and well."

"Is he a horrible person? Didn't he want me?"

Bev's shoulders drooped. "Oh, sweetie, just the opposite. Your father asked your mother if there was any possibility you were his."

She thought back to the journal entry. "You mean she never told him?"

"Your father was not only valedictorian of their class, but he also had a full ride to law school. He was going places."

"My father is a lawyer?"

"I'm not sure what happened to him after high school, but I know that was his plan. Your mom loved him, and she didn't want to hold him back."

"Shouldn't that have been his decision? Why is it my mother always thought she should make choices for everyone else? She was so selfish. I had a father this whole time? I grew up with problems because of my father's abandonment and you're telling me that was just another one of my mother's lies?"

Her aunt crossed her arms and bit her lip. "I'm so sorry. It wasn't my place to step in. I wasn't sure what to do."

"Do you know where he is now?"

"I'm not sure. I used to know where he lived. I can look into it more if you really want to know, that is."

Bev placed her hand on Kat's shoulder. She leaned her head against her chest and cried. "I'm so sorry, baby girl."

Her aunt held her close and patted her back. Aunt Bev was more of a mother to her than her mother ever was.

Bev grabbed her purse off the floor. "How about we get out of here? Are you hungry?'

She nodded.

"Then I have the perfect place I want to take you.

Ten

Ethan

He shivered in the chilly morning air, and the fish had yet to bite.

"How's that book writing coming along, Ethan? Ready to get a real job yet?" Brad laughed and took another sip of his hot coffee. Kevin laughed along with him.

He grinned, but they had no idea he made ten times more than the two of them put together. "It's going well. You know, it's a job."

Kevin began reeling in a fish. His pole bent and sank. "Looks like a big one."

"Hey, it's a giant northern pike."

Ethan netted the fish and lifted it into the boat. "That's quite the beauty. I have a feeling the biggest fish award has been claimed."

Kevin put down his pole and cracked open a beer from the cooler. "I could get used to this."

"You know, if you move out here with Lyndsey, you could fish a lot more. How is everything going with you two? Is Tracey still a problem?"

"We're good, and Tracey's out of the picture. Though she's still pretty upset I set her up. Your sister has been a saint about the whole thing."

"She can also be a pain in the butt."

"Of course, she's your sister. If she didn't get to you once in a while, I'd think something was wrong."

Ethan baited the line. "Have you not been together long?"

Kevin laughed. "We should have been together many years ago, but I'm an idiot."

Brad snorted. "I never knew what you saw in Tracey."

"I can't argue with that. She dug her claws in, and I fell for it years ago. By the time I realized who she really was, I was married to her."

"You're lucky you never knocked her up," Brad said with a grin.

"Kevin doesn't want kids, he's a sheriff. Too busy," Ethan said.

Kevin shook his head. "It wasn't that I never wanted kids. I just never thought it was the right time because I couldn't imagine having kids with Tracey. Can you imagine her being someone's mom?"

"So you're going to knock up my sister instead?"

They all laughed.

Kevin pulled a box out of his jacket. "She will have to say yes first." He showed them the ring.

"Wow. You guys have been together for a couple of weeks. You sure aren't taking it slow." Brad shook his head.

"Brad, you know our history. I know what I want, and I

won't let her slip away again. I want to start a family together, build a life with her. I never stopped loving her."

"You have a hell of a way of showing it." Brad moved closer to the ring and stared at it. "How much did this set you back? You know Lyndsey is a simple girl."

"She will love it," Ethan said, bringing it closer so he could examine it closely. "I saw this ring, and I knew it was the one."

"How are you going to top your brother and Victoria's wedding? That was unbelievable. The perfect beach wedding," Ethan said.

"It was. Although, it's not about the wedding, it's about the person, the marriage. Speaking of your sister and Troy, is it true they're moving here?"

"They were talking about it. My mom wants to sell, and they had a change in heart about travel. They want to take a break and live in Side Lake for a while."

Kevin nodded. "It would be great to have everyone living on the same road. Don't you guys tell a soul, or I'll kill you. Especially you, Brad." Kevin warned him. " Maddy can wait to find out until Lyndsey tells her, okay? I'm waiting until the time is right."

Brad put his hands up in the air in surrender. "My lips are sealed. I can keep a secret, can't I, Ethan?"

Ethan knew what secret he was talking about as the words left his mouth. He worried Brad would pressure them to spill the secret, but he was not paying attention. If Kat knew he told anyone, she'd really hate him. He wanted to get her to open up to him again. She was so good at the funeral, but after she ran out of the resort when she saw him, it killed him.

They unloaded the boat and built a fire on shore to warm up. Maddy and Lyndsey joined them shortly after.

"Where's Kat?" The words popped out of his mouth.

"I am going over there in an hour or so," Lyndsey said. "Her aunt was helping her sort boxes today. I'm giving them bonding time. Have you talked to her since... well since the cabin incident?"

Brad raised an eyebrow. "The cabin incident? What cabin incident?"

"It was nothing. Kat was keeping me company while I cleaned the cabin Ethan was staying in. When he got home from a run, he started flexing his muscles and scared Kat away."

Ethan jumped to his feet. "I did not flex my muscles. I was doing push-ups. I didn't know you guys were there."

"Wow. I want to hear the rest of this," Brad said, clinking his beer with Kevin. "How do you do push-ups without flexing, anyway?"

"Shut it, Brad. I didn't see them in there. It was my cabin, and I wasn't expecting anyone to be there." He glared at Lyndsey. "I came in after a run. I was all sweaty and didn't have a shirt on, and I started doing push-ups in front of the door. I didn't know they were there, or I wouldn't have done it."

Maddy put her head on Brad's shoulder and looked at Ethan. "Then what happened?"

"Kat froze and ran out the door at full speed," Lyndsey said.

"I didn't know your nakedness scared the chicks away," Kevin said, then he laughed.

Lyndsey hit him over the head with the book in her lap. "Really, Kevin?"

Brad shook his head. "I would have said it, but you beat me to it."

"Exactly. I was just saying what Brad was trying to say."

"And I'm being nice because she was scared off by those

abs of steel," Lyndsey said, playfully hitting him in the stomach.

Ethan sat down and took a sip of his beer. "I can't believe I'm going to say this, but I miss you guys giving me crap. It's really great to be back."

Ethan and Lyndsey were the last ones sitting by the fire as everyone else went off to bed.

Ethan leaned toward the fire. He cracked his knuckles and let out a deep breath.

"Alright, what's on your mind?" Lyndsey finally said.

"What do you mean?"

"Come on. You're shaking your legs, breathing hard, and hunched over with stress. I know what's on your mind. It's Kat, right?"

He rubbed his eyes and smiled. He leaned back in his chair to prove he was okay. "Yeah. Does she hate me?"

"I don't think she hates you, Ethan. I think she's confused and stressed. Nothing has changed since we last had this talk."

He nodded.

"You know, I never stopped wondering what was in that letter. Wait, don't answer that. Kat needs to tell me. I've tried to get it out of her, but her lips are sealed. I keep telling myself she has a reason."

How should he respond? "I want to tell you so bad, but I know it needs to come from her."

"Just tell me, is it that bad? I mean, it had to be a Dear John letter or something, I know that. Was it really such a big secret?"

He avoided looking at her or he might let it slip. He really wanted to get it out. "Yeah, it was, and it is."

· · ·

74

She crossed her legs and poked at the fire with a stick. "I don't understand why she didn't tell me. The only thing I can think of is that she was pregnant." She looked at him quickly, as if to read his face.

He kept a straight face, hoping not to give it away with his eyes or mouth or any facial expressions.

"She was, wasn't she?" She stared at him.

"Do you want me to tell you the truth?"

"No. I know it's the only reasonable explanation, but then I would have known if she had a kid. She couldn't hide it all these years if she had a teenager at home. Plus, where would her kid be right now? Unless..."

"Unless?" He repeated, hoping she would guess it right.

"Unless she didn't end up keeping the baby."

He stood up, his shoulders raised now. "We're going to get ourselves in trouble. I should go."

She nodded and looked down, but he saw the sadness in her eyes.

"Talk to her. Maybe she will tell you what the letter was about. You should know."

She nodded again, staring down at her hands. "I will. You know, Ethan, it's really great having everyone back together, even if it's just for a short time."

"It is, isn't it?" He took a step closer to her and squeezed her shoulder gently. "You're a great person, Lyndsey. I've always felt that way about you. I just want you to know that."

"Thank you. It's mutual." She forced a smile.

He turned to walk away and snapped his head back in her direction. "And Lyndsey. I'm not giving up on her."

"You know she has a boyfriend, right?"

He couldn't breathe. "What? Is it...serious?"

She shook her head and stood up. "I don't know. You'll have to ask her that question."

"Until I know for sure, I'll keep trying."

"I wouldn't expect anything less from you, Ethan."

He watched her walk back to her house until the darkness of the night swallowed her up, and he could no longer see her.

He was proud of himself for not telling her because it was obvious Kat never had.

Eleven

Kat

After dinner at the Viking, just four miles north of Side Lake, Aunt Bev dropped her off, and she dove right for the journal.

I feel hopeless. I can't seem to pull myself out of it. I know I'm supposed to write in my journal every day, but it's been too long since my last entry. I saw Him today. He came home for the holidays and was at Bimbo's. I was bartending, and he came to the bar and sat down in front of me. He was flirting with me, told me how much he missed me. I told him I was in a relationship. Ha! As if I'd ever be with another man when he stole my heart. I wanted to show him pictures of our baby, Kat. I wanted to tell him she has his eyes, that when she is really excited, she makes the same face as he does, smiling with her eyes. I wanted to tell him to stay, but I just couldn't. I love him so much and I want him to be happy and he'd be so hurt to know I never told him.

Last I heard, he was in law school, and I don't want this to impede his success.

Kat is attached to my mother. She follows her around the house and cries when she leaves. I think she can feel that my heart is broken and one day I worry she will think I don't love her. I do love her, I'm just broken. When he left, my heart went with him. I want to be a good mom. The only way I can survive each day is by numbing my pain with drinking. It works. I don't feel the pain as strong, and I can forget for just a moment that he's no longer here. My life is nothing. I don't have a thing going for me. I can't stop thinking about him. Why did I have to see him? As I sit here in my bedroom with a bottle of vodka, not even good vodka, just the cheap crap, all I can hear is the laughter of my baby girl and her grandma. It hurts. It hurts so bad. No one can help me. It hurts to know my baby girl would be better off without me, but I know it's true.

Kat bookmarked the page and closed the journal. Her heart could only read so much heartbreak, her eyes could no longer focus through the tears. Her mother had feelings and what broke her was letting go of the man she loved because she believed knowing he had a child would ruin his dreams. He should have been able to decide whether to stay or go. He should have had a choice. It may have changed everything. Did he still not know about her? Did her mother ever tell him, or did she die with her secret?

Resentment and anger sucked the air out of her lungs and squeezed her chest. Nausea overwhelmed her, and she held onto the wall for support.

All this time, she thought her mother had no emotions or

any feelings at all. She thought she was evil and never loved anything or anyone. She was wrong.

She stepped outside and breathed in the fresh air, as if that would help. She slowed her breathing and walked down the driveway. She needed to distance herself from the journal and the unhappy childhood memories that overwhelmed her.

To others, her childhood home seemed like a beautiful place overlooking the lake. To her, it was emptiness, and reminded her of the hard days with her mom after her grandmother died. Her grandmother was the one that took her down to the lake and taught her to skip rocks. She took her out in the canoe and taught her to swim in the lake. She is the one who taught her the true meaning of love.

Imagining her mother in any way other than the way she always remembered her—heartless and drunk--was difficult. She turned onto Greenrock Road and made her way toward CC Campground for an ice cream cone. Something she always did growing up with her grandmother. It was the one thing that would make her feel just a little better.

Nancy, the owner, smiled at her from behind the counter. "Hey, Kat. It's so great to see you back in Side Lake. Not exactly the best reason to visit, but the whole town has been talking about what a beautiful young woman you've become. Your mother was always bragging about you, you know."

Her mother bragged about her? She highly doubted that unless she was bragging to make her own life look better.

"Really?"

"Oh, yes. She said you were quite the social worker. You put your heart and soul into helping children and families. I know Lyndsey really struggled with it, but your mom said you are the best and you fight hard for their safety. She also said you have a strong mind and a big heart, and let me tell you, the one thing I know is those two things together is what makes you stand out among the rest."

"Thank you," she said. Did her mom really say all those things about her? Why did she never tell her that herself? Why did she never contact her at all?

She broke the silence. "Cookies and cream cone, please. On a sugar cone."

Nancy nodded and dug in.

"We're having a big BBQ tomorrow night for all the campers, and we'd love you to come if you're around."

She pushed a smile. "Thanks, but I've got my work cut out for me packing up my mom's house. She sure had a lot of stuff."

Nancy nodded at her with understanding and handed her the cone. Kat pulled out a five-dollar bill, but Nancy waved her off.

"No, no, this one is on me. It is so great to see you. Please don't be a stranger, and if you need any help over there with the cleaning or moving, just let me know."

"Thanks, Nancy," she said. The heaviness in her chest surprised her as she left. She had forgotten how caring Side Lake people were. Nancy was genuinely willing to help her, even though they had lost touch over the years.

When was the last time she even thought about the people at Side Lake? All she ever thought about was her mother and how much she despised her. She wasted so many years hating her and blaming her, yet it was so hard to shut it off.

She turned the corner to head to the road and was halted by a hard chest. She took a step back, eyeing the white ice cream with black cookies that now covered the man's white t-shirt. Her eyes moved up until his baby blue eyes locked with hers.

"Ethan?"

His mouth hung open. "Dang, that ice cream is cold."

"I'm so sorry, I didn't mean to—"

He laughed and wiped chunks of cookie off his shirt. "I'm sorry. I ruined your ice cream cone. Did you even get a bite?"

Why was he being so nice to her? She shook her head and threw her cone in the outside garbage.

"Let me get you another cone, okay?"

She couldn't speak, couldn't move. He went around her and came out minutes later with two cookies and cream ice cream cones in hand.

She took her cone. "I spill ice cream all over you and you buy me another one? I'm almost starting to believe you aren't a total jerk. Almost."

He grinned, and his eyes twinkled. "I don't want to give you the wrong impression of me. I was hoping you would say no so I could eat them both."

She stared deep into his eyes, trying to read him.

"Why don't we walk to the beach and eat our cones and you can remind me of all the reasons you think I'm such a jerk?"

She rolled her eyes but walked next to him, anyway. He was so annoying.

They walked the path in the woods that led to McCarthy's Beach.

"I don't want to make a habit of this, but I want to apologize for the way I acted the other day. I was in your cabin, and I was totally out of line for the way I treated you. I'm sorry. I don't know what got into me."

He stopped walking and held his chest with his free hand, overreacting to her apology. "You're apologizing to me? And here I thought you hating me was how we were going to bond forever."

She groaned. "You are impossible."

He laughed and grabbed her arm. "I'm just kidding. Kind of."

She turned away, and he laughed and jumped in front of

her. "I'm just kidding. Your mom just passed away, and I know you hate me for our history and whatever it is you think I did. I startled you. It's no big deal."

"You are to blame for our history, but as for the other day, I was in your cabin. It was my fault. I never should have been in your cabin without your permission, and I'm also sorry for the ice cream." She laughed and pointed at his shirt. "You wear it well."

He bit off a chunk of his ice cream. "It takes two."

"I hate how we left everything, but I had no time to process you being back here. My mother died and you and I have unresolved issues I didn't want to deal with. I just couldn't handle one more thing. That is on me, not you."

"Another apology? I feel like I don't know you at all," he said with a smirk, then his expression turned serious. "I didn't think about it that way. I just thought you hated your mom, and I should have thought more about how my going to her funeral would affect you."

"Stop doing that."

"What?"

"Trying to take the blame. Nothing has changed. I hated my mom and still do. I don't understand why it hurt me so much when she died."

He shook his head. "Because she was your mom. I think it's only natural to hurt a little."

She licked the bottom of her cone to stop it from dripping. "I never thought I'd end up back here and yet here I am. Crazy how life works sometimes."

They continued walking, and when their hands brushed together, Kat shivered in response.

"Is it as bad as you thought it would be?"

"What?"

"Coming back here."

She thought about that. Was he talking about him? About

being back for the funeral? "It brings back a lot of terrible memories."

"Oh," he said, looking deflated.

"Ethan, the only memories I have with you are amazing ones that ended up sad. My memories with you are not what kept me from coming back here, even if I'm still angry with you for how it ended and how you never tried to find me, but that's for another time."

He nodded. "I'll give you that, but I have to ask what happened to the ah... the ah..." He extended his arms over his stomach.

She laughed at how he struggled to say the words. She knew what he was asking, but she would cry if she talked about it right now.

"Can we talk about this some other time? It's been a long day, and I really want to have this conversation with you. I just don't know if I can right now."

His sad eyes crushed her, but she was not ready to talk about this with him yet. She never expected to run into him today, let alone have an emotional conversation with him. She needed time to prepare.

"Promise we will talk? It's been eating me alive for so many years."

"I promise," she said. "On a lighter note, tell me what really brought you back here? What have you been up to? Please distract me. I want to know what you've been doing all these years. Is there a Mrs. Ethan?" She raised a brow.

"There's no Mrs. Ethan, although there almost was, but we broke up."

"Why? I'm so sorry. What happened?"

Why did she want to know? She had a boyfriend, and she definitely did not care about his love life.

"It didn't work out. It's a long story."

She understood that. Relationships were complicated, and

she had her fair share. She would not push him. He'd tell her if and when he wanted to.

"To answer your question about why I'm here, I am a writer and I moved here to get some inspiration. Side Lake was always a place I felt solace, and I was really struggling to write until I got here. Now the words are flowing like they did back when I was still spending my summers here. I'm thinking about moving back here."

"So your words can keep flowing?"

He shook his head. "Not just that. Because I am happy here. I haven't been happy in so long. I almost forgot what it was like to truly be happy."

She lost her breath. Ethan was moving here? For good? A part of her wanted to stay just so she could get to know him again. Maybe he wasn't as bad as she thought he was. "What do you write about?"

"I write from the heart."

"I had no idea you were such a sucker for love," she said, her slow smile building.

"That's not exactly what I mean."

She went quiet, thinking about his writing. "Are you like a journalist?'

He shook his head. "Definitely not."

"Do you write books or magazine articles or something?"

He hesitated. "I write novels. Romance novels, to be exact."

She would not push him any further on the topic. He must be a struggling writer. Good for him for following his dreams. She couldn't imagine his love stories being very good, since he wasn't exactly Don Juan DeMarco.

"How about you? What were you doing in the cities? Lyndsey said you were a social worker or something?"

"Yeah, child protection, actually."

"Ooh, that doesn't sound like a simple job."

They sat down on the sandy beach and looked over at the lake. She heard the loons wailing in the distance. She took off her shoes and buried her toes in the warm sand. The beach was quiet, the sky overcast, but the air was warm.

"I enjoy it. I'm actually really good at it, but I'm just not sure I want to go back." She thought about the number of emails she would have to go back to and her body tensed at the thought. "Maybe I'll just sell my mother's house and take some time off before I figure out what I want to do next."

"So, you aren't staying then?"

Her leg shook and bumped his, causing instant goosebumps up her arms and her face grew hot.

"I never intended to come back, let alone stay and live here. It isn't my home anymore. It's funny because I ran so far, so fast after everything that happened."

"I'm so sorry about that, by the way."

"Don't be. My mom was evil."

"I never stopped thinking about you, you know," he whispered. "I wanted to find you, and I wanted to see you, but I also wanted to respect you by listening to the letter you left me."

Her eyes met his, and he forced a smile. "You're a big part of the reason I returned. Memories of us are everywhere around here. I just never in a million years thought you would actually be here."

He placed his hand on hers, and she shivered at his touch.

She shook his hand away. She would not go back there. No way. She'd moved on to a new life long ago. She needed to focus on getting him out of her head. She stood up and held her head high. "I should get going."

. . .

"I'll walk you."

She didn't protest.

They walked in silence until they reached the CC gas station.

"When should we meet? To talk about, you know, what happened?"

Her heart skipped a beat at the thought. She had put off this conversation for so long, convincing herself it was not the right time. But she needed to get this off her shoulders.

"How about tomorrow night? Pick me up at six and we can plan where we want to go."

He brought her hand to his lips and kissed it. "Thank you, Kat. Really. Thank. You."

She nodded and turned away. He waited long enough, it was time to tell him what happened.

Twelve

Ethan

When he got back to Pine Beach, the sun was high in the sky and the teenage girl he kayaked with was stacking firewood in front of his cabin. She was such a hard worker and strong considering her small size. She hardly looked like she was struggling to carry the heavy wood.

"Can I help you?"

She wiped the sweat off her face with her forearm and smiled at him. "Don't you have anything better to do than volunteer for hard labor?"

He loved her wit and sassy attitude.

"Not really."

She laughed and picked up another bundle.

"It looks like a great workout. Running every day isn't exactly the best for my old body."

"I don't think being in your thirties is very old, sir."

He grabbed a bundle off the trailer and carried it to the stack. "If you're calling me sir, you definitely think I'm old."

She hopped on a four-wheeler. "You're funny. Jump on if you aren't afraid of some hard work."

Five minutes later, they were in the middle of the woods, right off the four-wheeling trail. They stopped beside freshly chopped wood stacked in neat piles. They jumped off the side-by- side ATV and went to work, transferring all the wood onto the small trailer.

"Why isn't your brother helping?"

She laughed. "Dave is either working hard or disappearing into the woods to Snap his friends. He only does what he's told by my parents he has to do, and no more."

"So, you pick up the slack?"

"Of course."

Two hours later, the woodpile was replenished, and Emma gave him a bottle of warm water.

"I don't even get cold water?" He laughed and reached over to feel her warm bottle.

"Warm water is better for you. I never put bottles of water in the fridge. You should know that."

He was impressed.

Two high school girls came barreling at Emma from another camper.

"Em! Done working yet? Time for a swim."

"Yeah, just finishing up." She turned to him. "We're heading to the water trampoline and obstacle course out on the lake. In case you are done feeling old, come see if you can beat us."

"You're on."

He changed into his suit and by the time he got into the water, the kids were all on the trampoline. He walked out until the water was waist deep, then dove under. He swam with his head above the water because he forgot his goggles. His muscles were sore, but it felt good to stretch them.

He reached the obstacle course and pulled himself up on the inflatables. Next, he took on the climbing wall and then slid down the slide, his almost dry legs slowing him down. He dove into the water and swam

"Impressive," one girl said.

"I think I've hit my limit," he said to no one in particular.

He sat on the side of the trampoline as the girls jumped into the water. There wasn't a lot of bounce, but they did not seem to mind. A skier went by, pulled by a giant wakeboard boat.

He was about to dive into the water and head for shore when he spotted the birthmark on the back of Emma's neck. It was a red stork bite at the base of her head. He gasped.

Emma frowned. "What's wrong?"

He shook his head. "Nothing. I was just thinking you don't really look like your mom or dad."

"She was adopted when she was a baby," her blonde friend said.

"You were?"

"Yeah. I'm as pale as a ghost and my parents are both Italian. I thought everyone knew that."

"What about your brother? Is he adopted too?"

"No, my parents adopted me because they didn't think they could have any children and as soon as it was official, my mom became pregnant with my brother."

"That's crazy."

He thought back to when he was a teen and her parents, Mark and Amy, just had a baby and they got pregnant right away with Dave. He never suspected Emma was adopted. Nor did he think about the timeline for Kat's pregnancy. Was it possible?

That birthmark was too much of a coincidence. He looked over at Emma, but her low ponytail now hid the red circle from his view. It couldn't be. He needed to talk to Kat and ease his mind. Emma could not be their child, could she? The math was almost perfect. It had to be possible.

He tossed and turned until two in the morning. The resemblance between Emma and Kat kept invading his mind. Was he imagining the way her mannerisms reminded him of Kat? Her button nose and big eyes that looked just like Kat's? The shape of her lips that matched his, and that birthmark, the same birthmark Kat had. The same shape, even.

He jumped out of bed and dropped to the floor to clear his head and relieve his stress with some push-ups. He lost count once he hit fifty and fell the rest of the way to the floor, unable to get up. That's where he stayed until the sun found him on the floor. At six o'clock in the morning, he was ready to pound on Kat's door. He needed answers.

Kat's tired eyes were the first thing he saw when she opened her door.

"Ethan? Ethan, what are you doing here so early?"

"I'm sorry to wake you, but it's important. Can I come in?"

She rubbed her eyes and moved out of the way. "Is everything okay? You look upset."

"I'm trying to be patient, but I need to know what happened to the baby."

She gaped at him. "Excuse me?"

Why did he think showing up here without notice so early

in the morning would be a good idea? But he no longer cared. He needed answers.

"I know this is weird, and I never should have come this early in the morning, but I need to know." He ran his fingers through his hair, still wet from his sprint, but both running and push-ups failed to calm his nerves this time.

"It is weird. Can't this wait?"

She stared at him and when he did not reply, she dropped her hands to her side and let out an annoyed breath of air. She sat down on the couch.

He wanted to sit beside her, but his legs did not move.

"I tried to keep the baby, but my mom insisted she would be better off with someone else. I was only a teenager and not ready to raise a baby."

He hung onto the word she. Another clue, he may be right.

"Did you know my mom had me when she was a teenager?"

He shook his head. "No. I had no idea."

"Yeah, I ruined her life. So she insisted I have an abortion or give our baby up for adoption."

"I'm so sorry, Kat."

"Yeah, well, I had no choice."

"After I signed the adoption paperwork, I knew our baby was likely being adopted, but I always wondered what actually happened. Our baby was a girl?"

"Yes."

"I'm sorry I wasn't there for you. That must have been really hard for you to deal with on your own. My parents insisted I kept the secret. They wanted me to leave it in the past and never talk about it again. I tried to reach out and find you. A part of me always wondered if you kept her."

Her eyes teared up. "I had a closed adoption. My mom set

it all up. I never even held her when she was born or had a chance to name her."

He put his head in his hands. His heart beat rapidly as he listened to Kat. He wanted to tell her so bad, but what if he was wrong? Maybe she knew and she just hadn't told him yet.

"Do you know where she is? Who adopted her?"

She shook her head. "I found my mom's journal, and I was searching for answers. I don't want her to think I abandoned her. I want to explain. I must sound so stupid."

He wanted to wrap her up in his arms and take away all her pain. Should he tell her what he thought? What if he was wrong? He'd done enough by not being there for her. He should have tried harder. All those letters left unanswered. How many times had he tried to find her? If he told her his suspicions, would she believe him?

"You don't sound stupid at all. I can't believe your mother had a journal. I didn't know her well, but that doesn't sound like her."

She laughed through her tears. "It's not her. She started writing about it when she was pregnant with me. I'm not sure how long she wrote in it or if there are any answers, but it's just so hard to read."

He studies her. "What was it like, the day our baby was born?"

"It was the best and worst day of my life. I didn't get to hold her, Ethan. I didn't want to give her away, but I knew I had to. I want to find her and tell her who I am and that I love her. I want her to know I'm sorry for giving her up."

He sat down next to her and put his arm around her. She leaned into him and stopped, holding back the tears. She let out a loud cry, her body shaking beneath his arm. He wanted to take her pain away.

"Does anyone know?"

She shook her head. "Just my mom and my aunt knew."

Once she finally calmed down, he hugged her tight and lifted her chin so he could look into her beautiful eyes. Emma's eyes. But he needed to find out for sure before he told her.

"Thank you for telling me. My heart has been hurting for so long. To think I have a child out there somewhere that I never got to meet." There was no way she knew.

She pulled her feet up on the couch and hugged his torso, dropping her head in his lap.

They sat in silence as he rubbed her head. This felt so right. She felt so right. He wanted to be with her. Her breathing strengthened. She was out cold. He ran his fingers through her hair.

After all these years, he finally felt like this was what he was missing.

He nodded off, but woke up when his head started falling. He looked down at her, still snoring sweetly in his lap. He lifted her hair off her neck and saw the red blotch. Was this proof? Proof that their child was living in the same city they both left. He needed to find out for sure.

The door opened, and a man walked into the living room. Shock crossed his face as he stared at Ethan, then glanced at Kat.

The man's face reddened, and he clenched his fists at his sides. "Who the hell are you?"

"Who are you?" Ethan said. "Why did you come in here without knocking?"

"Kat's boyfriend. So why the hell is her head in your lap?"

His angry outburst woke Kat, and she jumped to her feet. "Andy, what are you doing here? I wasn't expecting you until tomorrow."

"It was supposed to be a surprise. I got off early," he said, through clenched teeth. "So, this is the notorious Ethan from your past, huh? Looks like he's in your present, too."

. . .

"It's not what it looks like."

She stumbled over her words.

Ethan just watched them both, confused.

Kat's eyes were red and swollen when she looked at Ethan and said, "You should go. We'll talk later. I'm sorry."

Andy crossed his hands in front of his body in an intimidating gesture. "Over my dead body the two of you are going to talk ever again."

Kat took the guy by the arm and led him into the other room while Ethan snuck out.

Her boyfriend? He forgot she had a boyfriend. She was back in his life and she finally opened up to him. Now her boyfriend had come back into her life like a plot twist.

His mind was spinning out of control at everything that had just happened. He ran the rest of the way home and did the one thing that helped him think and clear his mind other than push-ups.

He wrote.

And wrote.

And wrote.

And before he knew it, the moon replaced the sun outside his window, and his head was heavy. Another day had gone by, and four chapters were written.

He slept well for the first time in a long time, but he was mentally and emotionally drained, with no end in sight. Only more obstacles.

Thirteen

Kat

"I knew I should have come up with you. What the hell, Kat? The Ethan?"

"I'm sorry, but what you saw was nothing. I told him about our baby. That was a big deal for both of us. He's just a friend."

Andy dug his fingers into his eyes.

It was obvious he suspected there was more going on with her and Ethan then there was.

"You told me he didn't live here anymore. You told me he wouldn't be here. Is this why you insisted I work and didn't need to be here? Did you cheat on me?"

She knew what it looked like. The minute she arrived Lyndsey told her Ethan was here, and she knew she was doomed. Andy did not understand that she had unresolved issues with Ethan. She had to tell him about the baby. It was time. Some part of her knew Ethan would want her help find their daughter. And she desperately wanted to tell her daughter she cared, even if her daughter wanted nothing to do with her.

"I didn't know he was back. I promise, Andy. I wouldn't do that to you."

"Then why didn't you tell me when you found out? I've been calling you and you don't answer."

Her guilt turned to anger. "You know how hard it was for me to come back here. I had to plan my mother's funeral and host it. I didn't want to talk, I couldn't. Please, just let this go."

"Do you even want to be together anymore?"

She screamed at him, without even thinking. "I don't know! You need to trust me."

She wanted to be alone right now. She wanted him to let her be. She could not take any more of this conversation. She was mentally drained.

"You don't know?" His face softened. "I'm sorry, baby. I love you, and I do trust you. If you say it's nothing, then I guess I have to believe that."

She dug her palms into her eyes, and he reached out to comfort her. She shrugged off his hand and stepped away. "I just need to deal with all of this by myself."

"You don't mean that. I just got here." He looked devastated.

Did she mean that? Was she being unreasonable? She was no longer sure. What did she want? Her whole world had completely changed in the last few days. She needed to finish reading the journal, then find her father and her daughter. She could not do that with Andy around. He never understood her pain, nor was he part of her past.

"Just sleep in the guest room tonight. I'm too exhausted to talk about this right now, okay?"

"I'm not sleeping in a separate room, Kat. You do this and I'm gone."

He would get in the way and try to tell her what to do. He was playing games, and she did not have the patience to deal with him right now.

"Fine," she said, wiping her tears with the back of her hand. "You can sleep with me tonight, but tomorrow I can't promise anything."

"I'm your boyfriend. You can't just shut me out. We need to be there for each other."

"That's the problem, Andy. I need to deal with this by myself right now. You need to understand that."

She turned away, but he caught her by the shoulders and this time she did not fight it.

"If you think I'm leaving you alone with him, you're crazy. Not again, and you need me."

She was too tired to fight with him, too tired to convince him it was not about Ethan. Instead, she gave him a hug and whispered, "I'm going to bed."

He followed her up the stairs to her old bedroom. She went into the bathroom to change and brush her teeth and when she got out, his head was in her mother's journal.

"Is this your mother's journal?"

She ran at him, taking it from his hands. "Give that to me. Why do you do these things? This is why I wanted to be alone."

He put his hands up in the air to surrender. "You didn't even like her. Gosh, Kat, I don't know who you are right now."

Was she being unreasonable? Yep. Was she acting unusual? Yep. For once in her life, she was letting herself be who she was instead of being the person everyone wanted her to be. She was a people pleaser because her mother always made her feel like she was not good enough. She thought it was the only way people would like her, but now she couldn't care less. If people did not like her for who she was, that was on them.

For the first time, she was going to put herself first, and if Andy could not handle that, she would let him go before he pulled her back down. She was not settling for less.

She woke up in his arms and it felt comforting. She loved snuggling with Andy. He had a kind heart, and he was good to her. But she always had to reassure him. He had a horrible past just like hers, which made him very insecure at times. They met and stayed together because of their pasts.

The real question was, did she really love him or were they together because of convenience? He fought her battles for her. Stood up for her when she could not stand up for herself. She was always afraid people would dislike her. Was Andy what she really wanted?

She was so overwhelmed with decisions. She had made too many this week.

His chest felt so warm beneath her cheek. She glanced up at him. How could she hurt such a nice guy? She slipped out of bed and put on a sweatshirt. A walk was just what she needed to sneak away so she could think. She put on her shoes but left without a bra, in fear of waking Andy when she opened her dresser drawer.

Gently, she pulled the door closed behind her and made her way down the long, winding driveway. She kept glancing back to see if Andy was following her. Once she hit Greenrock Road, she knew he would never catch her. She walked at a quick pace, nearly running out of breath. Wow, was she out of shape? She stopped exercising when she found out her mother had died. She was too busy feeling down and depressed. Dealing with finding her daughter and her father, and seeing Ethan again, made her put off exercising.

The air was warm, and she was sweating, but her sweat-shirt hid her lack of a bra. A few cars passed her. One with a boat and another with a jet ski.

The burden of the gigantic house weighed heavily on her mind and in her heart. It seemed crazy, but the thought of her mother leaving her nothing would have been better than this. At least she had the diary. She could only hope all the answers were in there somewhere.

She headed toward CC Campground. When she was young, she dreamed of moving out of her mother's house and spending the summers in her own little camper, surrounded by friends and the feeling of a family.

She looked down McCarthy Beach Road, just over the bridge. She was so close to Ethan. She wanted to go to him, but that was unfair to Ethan and to Andy. She would lead Ethan on. Did he still have feelings for her after all these years? No. He didn't. He just felt bad for her, and he probably hated her for cutting him off. But he wrote off their child. This was not her fault.

Her feet had a mind of their own as she walked down the dirt road at Pine Beach. She could say she was looking for Lyndsey. Sure, Lyndsey was not working this morning, but would they know she knew that?

She held her head high, confident. She went down to the beach and out onto the dock.

"You can't walk right on by and not stop to say hello," a familiar voice said behind her.

"Ethan?"

"You seem so surprised."

He grinned and butterflies fluttered in her stomach. "I...I thought you'd be mad at me after Andy showed up and I kind of booted you out. I'm so sorry. I just—"

. . .

"No need to apologize. I knew you had a life after me. I'm glad I got to spend some time with you before I met him in person and had to come to terms with the fact that he is, in fact, a real person. I forgot how easy it was when it was just us."

Being with him was easy and wonderful, as if no time had passed. Did he feel it too?

Footsteps echoed off the dock. A teenage girl headed their way. Kat looked away, then turned back to get another look at the young woman. Her breath caught in her throat, and her heart thumped against her chest. Who was this girl? Why did she look so familiar?

"Hi Ethan, I thought you were up. I'm getting ready to paddle board if you want to join me. My brother won't get his butt out of bed to come with me." She looked at Kat as if just noticing she was standing there. "Oh, hello. I'm Emma."

Kat tilted her head to the side. "You look so familiar. Do I know you?"

Emma giggled and raised her hand. "You must be Ethan's childhood girlfriend. Kat, right?"

Kat shot Ethan a confused look, and he bit his lip, his cheeks turning a light shade of red. Does a strong, gorgeous man like him get embarrassed? What had he said to this girl about her? She shook off the questions, trying to control her overthinking.

"I don't think we've met. I don't remember you, anyway. Did you stay here before?"

She stared blankly at the beautiful young woman. The last time she had been at Side Lake was before this young woman was even born. Unless she randomly ran into her in the cities, they had not met.

She shook off the thought. "No. You must just look like someone I know. It's a small town. I'm sure I see your mom in you."

The girl seemed to freeze. What did she say that made her

this upset? She thought back to her teenage years. She never wanted to be told she looked like her mother. She hated when people said that, especially since it was not true. She looked nothing like her mother, and sometimes she dreamed her mother was not her real mother.

"I was adopted, so I don't know what my mom looks like."

A passing boat created vast waves that hit the shore and covered the sound of her fast heartbeat. Her lungs squeezed inside her chest. She looked at Ethan and his eyes confirmed he knew exactly who she was.

How long had he known? Why didn't he tell her? Was this her dose of karma? Why was she the last to know?

Her knees buckled beneath her, and Ethan dove forward to catch her. Her body was numb, and she had no control.

It's me, your mother. Please don't hate me.

But she could not speak. Her traitorous tongue would not move.

She closed her eyes and when she finally had the strength to open them, she was in Ethan's arms. Carried by him as if she was his bride, again. She closed her eyes, not wanting to think about anything. This was right where she needed to be.

In his arms.

Fourteen

Ethan

"What's wrong with her? Does this happen often?"

Emma peeked from behind him and asked question after question about why Kat had collapsed. How could he tell Emma that Kat had figured out what he'd known for a few days? But Kat knew the minute their eyes met. Motherly instinct.

"I think she has low blood sugar. Would you mind getting her some crackers and a glass of juice from the kitchen?"

She nodded her head, still struggling to pull her gaze away from Kat.

Kat's eyes fluttered and then opened. Confusion set in. "Ethan? What—what happened?"

"You passed out. Are you okay? Does anything hurt?"

She felt her head. "I don't think so. Is that...am I dreaming? Was that really her?"

Emma came running into Ethan's bedroom. She held a glass of juice and some crackers in her hand. "Here you go."

Kat's hands rose to cover her face. "I thought I was dreaming."

"Nope, just low blood sugar," he said, but it came out flat, unconvincing.

"Oh."

"Are you sure I shouldn't call an ambulance or get my parents or something?" Emma said.

"NO!" Ethan and Kat said in unison.

Emma backed away.

"She'll be fine. You can go paddle boarding, Emma. I'll stay with Kat and let her rest for a bit."

"You sure? I don't mind—"

"No, really, I'm fine. This happens all the time."

Emma walked away with a wave. Kat's eyes followed Emma's every move as if she was watching her take her first steps. Something they both missed.

Once she was gone, Ethan swiped away a few strands of hair on her forehead. "It's unbelievable, isn't it?"

Kat sat up fast and sent Ethan flying to his feet.

"What?"

"You knew? You knew she was our daughter, and you didn't tell me?"

She raised her chin, and her lips curled.

"I wasn't sure how to tell you. What if I was wrong? I had to make sure before I said anything."

She glared at him. "How could you possibly think you were wrong? How long have you known? Is this why you're back?"

He waved his hands. "No, no, no. It's not like that at all. I was at the lake with her and I saw how familiar she looked and her birthmark—"

"Does she know you know? Does she know about me?"

"No. I don't know. I don't think she knows anything. She's never let on she knows who I am. She knows she was adopted, but I don't think she has any idea who her real parents are."

Her hands were now in fists. "I can't believe you didn't tell me."

Was she really mad at him or was she hurt that their daughter was at Side Lake the whole time without her knowing? He was pretty sure he knew the answer.

"I need to go. I can't do this right now."

Tears lingered in her eyes. He wanted to grab her and hold her, hug her tight, so she could cry on his shoulder. But she was angry and hurt and she'd probably punch him for not letting her go. She was in shock, and she needed to process this.

Kat opened the cabin door, slammed it, took two steps, and then came back to the door and opened it. Her eyes reflected shock.

"What happened? Did you forget something?"

She exhaled and sobbed into her hands. Her shoulders shook. He pulled her into his arms. She tried to fight him at first, but all at once her body collapsed into him and she wept into his shoulder.

Their bodies drew together, and it felt so right, touching her, hugging her, loving her. All these years, he still felt the same way. Was he crazy? They were so young when they were torn apart, like Allie and Noah. How many times had he watched *The Notebook* and thought about Kat? That book motivated him to write his first novel.

His mind raced as he held Kat close, and strong emotions he kept hidden took over his body. She was the reason he was writing again, and she was the reason he came back. Sure, she hadn't been living here, but the memories of her were all around him and they inspired him again.

He would not let her go. Not without a fight. His biggest fear was Kat leaving again, but he knew she would not leave, not when their child was in Side Lake.

Her crying slowed, and she pulled away to wipe her tears with the back of her hand. "I tried to leave, but she was standing outside and I couldn't bring myself to talk to her. It was just too much. I don't even know what to say."

"Take all the time you need. You don't need to know what to say."

"Is it stupid? I've been dreaming about her for so many years. I had everything rehearsed, and then I see her in person, and I literally black out. What's wrong with me?"

He wrapped his arms around her again and squeezed her. Her head tucked in beneath his chin.

"There is nothing wrong with you. I think you're in shock. Before we say anything to her, we need to talk to Mark and Amy. It's the right thing to do."

"But she's our daughter, Ethan," she pleaded.

"Hey, hey, I'm not trying to be mean. I just, well, she has other parents who raised her, and from what I've seen of Emma, they've done a fabulous job. Out of respect, we can't turn her world upside down without telling her other parents."

She leaned her head into her fist and finally said, "But she's ours, Ethan. She's ours, right?"

"Of course, she is, but she doesn't know us yet. Her parents can help. She will always be ours."

Kat sniffed. "I don't believe you. You just don't want her to know about us, do you? You don't want to be her father."

"That's not it at all, Kat. I want to tell her, but we need to take the proper steps."

"Oh, Ethan. Don't pretend you care. You couldn't even tell me my child was right here. You knew how much it meant to me."

"I—" He couldn't find the words to defend himself.

"I'll figure this out on my own. I don't need your help."

She left before he could say another word. Was it true? Was he being too cautious? Did he come off like he didn't care? Kat was hurting and pushing him away. He had to get her to talk to him, but right now he needed to write and give her some time to cool off.

He had no choice.

When he wrote, time flew by. The characters took over his mind. He always pictured the same woman in his stories, even when he described her in different ways. She was the love of his life all this time. The main character was always Kat.

Fifteen

Kat

She slammed the front door and stomped her way to her mother's journal. She opened the box, but the journal was no longer there. Did she move it? Did she forget it in her room? She tried to think back. No, she specifically remembered putting it in the box when she was cleaning. Or did she put it in one of the boxes with the donations? She ran to the garage and pulled the boxes apart.

"Is everything okay?"

Andy stood behind her. Concern was written all over his face.

She laughed. "Yeah, I lost something. I must look crazy."

"What did you lose?"

Was that a guilty look on his face? No. Had he taken the journal? She yelled at him when she saw him reading it that day. She was just being paranoid.

"My mom's journal. Have you seen it?"

"If you hadn't hidden it from me, I would know where it is. I'll help you find it."

He kneeled down next to her and opened another box.

She did not want him to find the journal and read it. She didn't want his help at all.

Her mother's secrets were her secrets, and she did not want to share them with him. Letting him in on that part of her life made her feel uncomfortable. But she should want to share her feelings with the man she loved. Maybe she needed to let him in. She owed it to him.

"Andy, why don't we go out for dinner? I don't feel like we've had any time together. I've been distant and on edge since you arrived, and I'm sorry. I can find the journal tomorrow. Right now, I want to have some time with you."

He put his arm around her. "That sounds amazing. Are you sure?"

She got to her feet. She felt guilty for suspecting he stole her mother's journal in the first place. "I'm sure. Just let me change quick and I'll take you out for the best pizza and wings you have ever had."

"That sounds perfect." He lifted her up and kissed her gently.

Why didn't she feel anything? She had to be too stressed to feel anything. She loved him. He came all the way here to check on her. They'd been through so much together.

She needed a distraction to take away the emotions from today. She wanted to tell Andy about meeting her daughter, but saying it out loud was too hard. She would tell him as soon as she spoke to Mark and Amy at the resort. She knew them well when she was young. They were so good to her and let her hang out all the time at Pine Beach. They were so kind. They wouldn't be upset that Emma's biological parents wanted to get to know her, would they? Maybe Ethan was right, maybe they wouldn't be okay with this. Maybe they needed to talk to her parents first.

In the summer, Bimbo's was full of Side Lake summer people who were boating on the lakes all day, with their windblown hair and damp swimsuits under t-shirts and jeans. Table talk was loud and joyful and this was the place to be.

Bimbos took her back to the happy times in her childhood with her friends and their families, out for dinner after a day in the sun. There was live entertainment and a game area for the children to play. The owners were always friendly, and the pizza was the best around.

Andy pointed at a small table in front of the stage, and they quickly made their way before someone beat them to it. He pulled out her chair and she sat down, looking around for familiar faces. Only a couple of tables had people she knew sitting at them. The summers in Side Lake were filled with more tourists or those who spent their summers at their cabins than locals.

"It smells amazing in here," Andy said. His eyes followed a waitress carrying pizzas to the table next to them. "That looks so good."

"It tastes even better than it looks," she said. "And over there is where we had the brunch for my mother's funeral." She pointed to the room that went off to the side.

"I feel terrible that I wasn't here."

She shook her head. "Don't be. I really meant what I said. I needed some time to process this all, you know?"

He opened the menu and stared down at it. "I know. But I should have come, anyway. I hate I wasn't here. Was Ethan at the funeral?"

It was only a matter of time before he asked her. "Yes, he came."

He shook his head, and she took a drink of water to avoid seeing the hurt look in his eyes.

He put his hand on hers. Before he could say anything, the waitress came to their table.

"Oh, hey! Kat, right? I'm so glad you came in. I hope you're feeling better. You gave me quite a scare this morning when you blacked out like that. So scary."

She choked on her water and coughed. Emma. She did not know her daughter worked at Bimbo's.

"Are you feeling better?" Emma asked.

No. Not one bit. This was not what she needed tonight. What could she say to Emma? She took another drink of her water to help the coughing stop and to delay her response.

"Kat, you passed out this morning? What happened?" Andy said, looking genuinely concerned.

She shook her head. "No big deal. Just a little heat exhaustion and low blood sugar."

What if he saw the similarities between them? What if he figured out who she was? She was not ready for this. He could blow everything right now.

"That seems like a pretty big deal," he said, with a disappointed shake of his head.

"Oh, hi, I'm Emma," she said, shaking Andy's hand. She turned back to Kat before Andy had a chance to reply. "You're so lucky Ethan was there to catch you. He's such a good guy. Where is he tonight, anyway? I'm surprised he's not joining you."

Oh crap.

She felt Andy's eyes burning through the side of her head, but she pretended not to notice. "Yeah. Well, I guess we should probably order so you can get back to your other tables. I know it's a busy night."

. . .

"I'm just glad you are feeling better. What can I get for you?" Emma took out her notebook and held it in front of her.

"A large George's Special, and we'll take an order of the boneless hot wings," she said. Perhaps she could pretend this conversation never happened. Her daughter could not find out that Andy was her boyfriend. She and Ethan looked cozy and had been spending too much time together at Pine Beach. She knew what this might look like to Emma.

"What do you have on tap?" Andy muttered, his cold eyes not leaving Kat's face.

Kat grabbed her napkin and fidgeted with it on her lap.

Guilty, and she would never hear the end of it.

"We have Summit—"

Andy sniffed dismissively and did not look at the waitress. "A Minnesota beer. I'll have that. Thanks."

"This water is fine for me," she said before Emma even asked.

"Okay, I'll be right back with that then," she said with narrowed eyes before she turned and walked away.

Andy crossed his arms and cleared his throat loud enough to be heard over the surrounding conversations.

"It's not like it sounds."

He tilted his head and scrunched up his face. "Oh, really. Then how did it sound?"

The situation was impossible. Nothing she said would be the right answer. She was there with him, but she had no way of answering him without telling him the truth, and she was not ready for that.

"Well." he said, a little louder this time.

"Not good."

He got up from the table and walked to the bathroom. She put her head in her hands and looked down.

"Kat?"

Lyndsey stood next to her at her table. "Are you alright?"

Was this seriously happening right now?

"Yeah, just tired."

"I heard you passed out today. Are you sure you're okay?"

Seriously? Was there a town meeting she missed? People sure loved to gossip. Her blood boiled, but when she opened up her mouth, she made eye contact with Maddy standing beside Lyndsey, and her heart fell. She had not seen Maddy since she passed out and was taken by ambulance to the hospital. Her eyes filled with tears at the memory. All her troubles faded, and she jumped up to hug her.

"Maddy! It's been so long!"

Maddy pushed past Lyndsey and hugged her tight. "Kat. It's so good to finally see you. I'm so sorry I never got to see you at your mother's funeral. David wasn't feeling well so I couldn't make it to the wake, then I went to the luncheon, but David started puking and I had to leave before I even had time to tell you how sorry I am."

She shook her head, still holding onto Maddy. "Don't feel bad. I'm so glad to see you. How are you? Little David? I can't believe it. I'm so happy for you."

She felt a tap on her shoulder, and her whole body tightened while her excitement extinguished.

"Maddy, Lyndsey, meet my boyfriend, Andy," she said.

The introduction was more for his benefit and hopefully forgiveness than it was for Maddy.

Maddy smiled brightly and took Andy's hand, giving him a handshake. "Nice to meet you. Your girlfriend saved my life, you know?"

His eyebrow raised. "Oh?"

"She told you she saved my life, didn't she?"

He had a blank look on his face. "I don't think she did."

"Sounds like Kat. So humble."

Maddy smiled at her, then turned back to Andy. "I met her at the Turtleman Triathlon in Shoreview a couple of years ago. We both knew Lyndsey and decided to race together, since Lyndsey would only run if a wolf was chasing her."

Lyndsey laughed. "So true."

"I was running, and I passed out. Your girlfriend stopped running to help me and jumped into the ambulance with me. I did not know I was pregnant with my son David at the time. She's an angel. You're a lucky guy."

Andy just stood there.

Heat rose up Kat's neck. She was not good at compliments and did not know how to respond.

Brad pushed past his wife and gave her a warm hug. "Kat. Hello again. So sorry for your loss. If there's anything you need at all, just let us know. You need to come down and hang out with all of us like the old days. We have the hot tub up, and we still have a few weeks left of summer for skiing. It'll be fun."

Kevin stepped forward next. "It's been years. I'd love to see you on skis again. I've seen no one ski quite like you and Lyndsey."

Andy scowled. "You ski?"

Andy was angry. Why? "Not for a while. Kevin's embellishing a bit."

"No, I'm not. You're just being humble. Come on, Kat, get back on them. You're talented," Kevin said with his hand on her shoulder.

"Well..."

"I'm not taking no for an answer. You two are coming out on the boat like the old days," Brad said.

She avoided looking at Andy for fear of his reaction. She never told him she skied. She left all that behind her when she left Side Lake. But she was back and the thought of skiing again excited her. Would it be easy to get back up after all this time? She loved the water, and at one time had thought she would live near water forever. Andy would understand eventually. He had to.

"Ethan's over there saving us a table. Have you guys eaten? You should join us," Maddy said.

Ethan was here, too? This really was a disaster.

"I think—"

Andy cut her off. "We'd love to, right, honey?"

She glanced in his direction, and he raised his eyebrows at her with a challenging look. "Wouldn't we, Kat?"

She looked at her friends and back at him again with a forced smile. She leaned over and whispered, "Are you sure? We don't have to."

"I insist," he said.

He was challenging her, but she was in no mood to play games.

"Okay, I guess we'll join you then. I'll let the waitress know."

She turned toward the waitress station, but remembered why this was a bad idea.

"Actually, Andy, would you mind telling the waitress? I need to go to the ladies' room."

The look in his eyes was not one of joy, but she left before he denied her request.

On her way out of the bathroom, she almost collided with Ethan again.

"Ethan? What are you doing in the hallway?"

"I wanted to apologize. I'm sorry for the way everything went down earlier."

She forgot how good looking he was. He was wearing Brooks because he was always running. Her eyes skimmed back up his legs, because they had to get back to his face somehow, but not without noticing his tight faded jeans and the blue cardigan sweater that hugged his strong arms and buttons that covered up the abs she drooled over just a few days ago.

She wanted to rip those buttons off. What was wrong with her? How inappropriate. Ethan did not feel that way about her, and she was with Andy. She was once again distracted by the way his jaw was clenching and the muscles on his jawline were bulging. She needed to quit staring at him and stop letting her mind wander like this.

Her heart fluttered when their eyes met.

She glanced behind them to make sure Emma was not around. "Don't apologize. Listen, my boyfriend doesn't know about, you know, our...um, you know," she whispered. The word daughter would not come out.

He nodded, not hiding the fact that he was staring at her lips as she talked and then back into her eyes. How does he do that? How does he make her feel like a giddy teenager with just a glance? Like the most beautiful person in the world, in his eyes.

"Okay. I won't say anything. Don't worry about that."

"Don't tell anyone," she said sternly. "Oh, and—"

Before she finished, Kevin strolled down the hallway toward the bathroom, a curious brow raised in their direction.

"Hi," she said, and made her way past him.

Sometime soon, they would all discover how she and Ethan were hiding a daughter. The thought made her nauseous.

Sixteen

Ethan

He made his way around the waitress, who just happened to be his biological daughter, and walked to the end of the table by the wall. His friends took all the outside seats and left him the farthest seat, which was hard as heck to get to.

Emma came to the table. "Ethan? I was just telling Kat that it's weird you weren't here with her. You two are connected at the hip.,"

Did Kat know Emma was our waitress? Everything about her was so perfect. Of course, it was. She was a spitting image of her mother. He analyzed everything about her. What features she got from her mother, and which features she got from him? She was his baby. Well, grown-up baby, but still the same. He wanted to run up and hug her, tell her how sorry he was. He was so dumb to sign that paperwork. How could he agree to give up being her father? He was young, dumb, and selfish.

"I didn't realize you worked here, too," he said, purposely avoiding her question. Maybe she would get the hint and not to keep talking about him and Kat in front of her boyfriend. He may want Kat back, but embarrassing Andy was not the right way to go about it. "You keep busy."

Of all the things he could have said.

Kevin shook his head at him.

Ethan cleared his throat, wanting to distract her from what he just said. "Emma, can I get a water and a Colorado Bulldog, please?"

Kevin shot him a sideways glance.

"What? I'm not driving."

Kevin shook his head.

"Coming right up," she said. "Are you all ready to order?"

After they all ordered and she left the table, Kevin leaned toward him. Everyone was having their own side conversations and not paying attention to them.

"Are you going to tell me what's going on with you and Kat?" He looked away and leaned toward Ethan again. "Scratch that. I'm not sure I want to know. Just promise me if there is anything going on between the two of you, you won't break her heart. Lyndsey will kill me, and Kat can't take anymore right now."

Ethan leaned toward him, but his eyes were on the table to make sure no one could eavesdrop. "I promise you, if she was mine, I would be the one protecting her heart, not breaking it."

Kevin gave him a nod of understanding.

"So, Ethan, I've heard so much about you," Kat's boyfriend said from down the table.

Ethan glanced at Kat, but she looked down.

"Oh, yeah?" This was uncomfortable since he had to talk loud enough to be heard over the two people between them and all the surrounding noise.

"Not really. She just said you had a pretty big crush on her when you were kids. That's so cute."

Jealous much? Or was this some kind of ploy for Andy to try to intimidate him?

"Yeah, well, we were very close back then."

"Hmm."

The waitress came back with their drinks and saved him from the questions, though this was nowhere near the end of it. Hopefully, he'd give it a rest for now so they could all enjoy their food.

"Tell us about yourself, Andy, is it? How long have the two of you been together?" Brad asked.

Andy put his arm around Kat's shoulder, no doubt reminding Ethan who she belonged to. That she was his.

He looked at Kat. "We met what, five years ago now?"

Kat nodded.

"Kat's aunt was my neighbor, and I fell in love with Kat the moment I met her."

Oh, puke.

"Kat was cutting down a tree with an axe on our property line. She didn't know she was actually on my side."

"And he was very vocal about that," Kat said, with a laugh. "It definitely wasn't love at first sight." She leaned into the table and loudly whispered, "We hated each other."

"I didn't hate you. I was just pissed you were cutting down my family tree."

Maddy spoke up, "Family tree?"

"Yeah. She didn't realize my family had a tree swing on the other side of that tree. It had been around for generations, since my grandma was a little girl."

They all gasped and laughed. Ethan pretended to laugh along with them, but he really wanted to change the subject. Last thing he wanted to hear was how they met or how in love they were.

Kevin stood up at the table. "Who wants to play pull tabs?"

"I will," Brad said, pushing his chair back. "Ethan? Andy?"

Ethan waved him off, but Andy stood up with them. "I'm in. How much?"

They all headed to the bar for pull tabs, leaving the girls and Ethan at the table.

"So, Ethan, what do you do all day in that cabin, anyway?" Maddy asked.

"I write a lot and exercise. Taking advantage of the lake life, I guess you could say."

"That's right. Lyndsey tells me you like to do push-ups," Maddy said, her tight lips trying but failing to hide a smirk. "Isn't that right, Kat?"

Lyndsey slapped her on the arm. "Really?"

"What? I think it's funny."

His face grew hot. The table vibrated, but he did not realize at first it was his phone until Maddy said, "You going to answer that?"

He picked up his phone, and Zoey popped up on the screen.

Brad came behind him and looked over his shoulder.

"Ooh, who is Zoey?"

"I need to take this."

He answered the phone and made his way outside. "Zoey, what's up? Why are you calling so late?"

"The publisher loves your new book! It's a big contract. I'll send it over to you. This is the best book you've written in ten years. Ethan, I didn't know you had so much heart. Northern

Minnesota is good for you. Congratulations, you're back. The lake really inspires your creativity. I should never have doubted you."

Kat was good for him. She was the reason his writing was good ten years ago and why his writing was back. Because he still loved her. No longer did he lust over her. He loved her.

"But..."

"Oh no, what's the problem, Zoey? Don't tell me they want me to come back to New York."

"No, it's not that. They want you to go on a book tour and they mentioned making it into a movie shot on location in Side Lake."

He exhaled. "I told you I'm not revealing who I am yet."

"Ethan, you have to, she pleaded. "Trust me on this, it's time. What is it you're so scared of? You deserve recognition for all you've done. They want to do a big reveal on *Good Morning America*. You should be ecstatic."

Good Morning America? This was huge, but not his style. Few people knew who he was. What would Kat say? What would she think? He'd scared her away before he had a chance to get to know their daughter and before she got to know him better and hopefully fell back in love with him. She felt the spark, she had to feel the spark. Every time they touched, he felt it.

"If you don't do it, they said they aren't publishing your book. I know you have other options, but you aren't getting a deal like this again."

"I'm not doing it, Zoey, he said sternly. "You know how I feel about this."

She was silent for a moment before finally saying, "Will you please think about it? I'll give you a week, but promise me you'll keep an open mind? This is everything you wanted. You're a good-looking single guy. There's no doubt the ladies will go crazy over you."

He pinched the bridge of his nose, then looked over the lake in front of him.

"I'll think about it, okay?"

"Thank you. You're going to be a very rich man, Elizabeth Conrad. A very rich man. Mark my words."

"Yeah, so you say." Money wasn't his issue.

"Have a wonderful night, and I'll call you next week."

He hung up the phone and walked across the street to the dock, and sat down at the end. He took off his shoes and dangled his feet in the water. The chilly breeze off the lake sent a chill through his body, but it was refreshing. His stomach growled. He needed a minute with nature before he could go back inside and face them all.

"Ethan, is everything okay?"

Kat stood behind him. He jumped to his feet and put on his shoes.

"Yeah, it's fine. I just needed a minute and had to take a quick call."

"Was that your girlfriend? Was she checking in on you to make sure you weren't causing any trouble?"

"I guess I can ask you the same question. Won't your boyfriend be angry when he finds out you're out here with me?"

"I'm sorry about him. He can be a lot sometimes. Andy knows about our history and that we have a child. He can't have kids, so it's a sore subject. Lost a testicle jumping over a fence."

"Are you serious?"

She laughed. "Yeah, he was like ten years old. The other one was damaged pretty bad, but he still has one, it just doesn't work."

121

He shook his head. Picking on Andy's misfortune was not who he was.

"TMI, but that sounds painful."

She shrugged. "Anyway, I've been thinking about what you said. I want to talk to Mark and Amy about our um.... daughter."

She had a hard time saying the words, and he understood completely. Knowing they had a grown-up daughter was crazy. Plus, she was working beyond the walls of the restaurant, unaware they were her biological parents. Their secret was the hardest thing he'd ever had to keep.

"I'd like that. I didn't mean to step on your toes, and I'm sorry if it came off that way, but I don't want to scare her away."

She walked two steps to the edge of the dock, her back to him. "What if they say no?"

He took a step forward and wrapped his arms around her and put his head on her shoulder. They watched the sunset on the horizon. It was so beautiful here. Why did he stay away so long? Because she was gone so long, he had no reason to come back and be reminded of what he lost.

"Let's not worry about that unless we have to. We'll take it one step at a time." He leaned in and kissed her cheek. His lips were warm from the touch.

She shivered and wrapped her arms around his neck. Gazing into his eyes, she whispered, "Why can't I stop thinking about you?"

Her words sent a thrill up his back.

She sighed. "I better go or I'll be in trouble."

She dropped her hands and slowly graced past him. "I'll come over tomorrow, early in the afternoon, then we can come up with a plan to tell them the truth."

He nodded. They walked back to Bimbo's together. He forced himself not to touch her, but their bodies were like magnets. He touched her lower back after he opened the front door and followed her in. She was so beautiful it hurt.

He hesitated. "Should we walk in separate?"

"Nah, Brad and Andy are at the bar taking shots. They took a pizza to the bar. He thinks he can out drink Brad. He does not know how hard it is to keep up with an Iron Ranger."

"Isn't that the truth?"

He followed her, leaving some distance behind her in case her boyfriend was not drunk enough yet. He would not be the person who broke them up. Kat needed to decide this on her own, and he needed to keep his hands to himself.

Seventeen

Kat

When the name Zoey popped up on Ethan's screen, Kat got up and followed him outside. Did he have a girlfriend? Why was he actually in Side Lake? Did Zoey live in the area? Was she back in New York? Wait, was this jealousy? It left a bitter taste in her mouth.

She had not planned on him seeing her, but he looked so sad when he got off the phone. Was she feeling a bond with him because they shared a daughter?

Now they were back in the restaurant, eating pizza and laughing. The boys were still at the bar taking shots and doing pull tabs, and Ethan was sitting next to her. The way his knee kept gracing hers made her tremble.

Maddy opened her mouth to speak, and Kat did not know what would come out of her mouth next. She was much sassier than she realized.

"So, the two of you were madly in love as teenagers until you moved to the cities, right?"

Maddy was not from Side Lake so her curiosity was justified.

"Yes, we were madly in love until my mom caught us having sex," Kat said, the vision still so vivid in her brain. She thought her mother was going to castrate Ethan.

"You should have seen him run with his pants around his ankles. An image I'll never forget."

Ethan choked on his beer and started laughing. "You ever meet her mom? She was very intimidating."

"So, you guys just stopped talking until now when you both happened to return to Side Lake at the same time? Sounds like a love story in the making."

True, the coincidence was unnerving. They both returned to the lake within days of each other. Although her visit was not planned and it was not a love story.

Ethan answered for both of them. "There were a lot of obstacles in the way, so it was definitely quite the coincidence. We had no way to communicate. She left me a letter and then she was gone. Her mom made sure we could not contact each other."

"That's so sad," Maddy said. "It's ironic you both came back after all these years of being away."

"We have a lot of unfinished business, but that was a long time ago. We're just friends now.," Kat said, and she really wanted to believe it.

"Now she's happily taken by a better man," Andy said, his eyes challenging Ethan.

She cringed at his words. He sat down next to her and landed a kiss on her lips.

She smiled and glanced at Ethan. He turned away quickly. Had he noticed the kiss?

Andy grabbed Kat's hand and glared at Ethan. "What made you return to the area after all these years, Ethan?"

He was slurring his words. He was drunk and had spent a small fortune on pull tabs and booze. What a jerk. He was trying too hard to fit in with the guys. She needed to get him out of there before he made a fool of himself.

"The lake is the place I grew up in the summers. It's where I found my peace," Ethan said. "I'm a creative so I like the peacefulness of it all. New York changed after COVID. I changed after COVID. I realized the busyness of New York was not where I wanted to be anymore. You could say I grew up."

"I'm not sure about that," Andy said under his breath, but loud enough for everyone to hear.

"Anyway," Lyndsey said. "How's the packing going, Kat? Can I come over and help you tomorrow? I'd love to spend some time with you before you leave, and I'm great at organizing."

Lyndsey to the rescue.

"Yeah, that would be great. Thank you. You don't have to do that, you know. You've done so much already."

"I want to," Lyndsey said sweetly.

"Can I help, too?" Maddy squeezed Kat's arm. "Brad can hang out with David and we'll have some girl time. Then we can spend the day at the lake, and you guys can catch me up on all your lake stories from your teenage years."

Despite all the years she had been gone, Lyndsey was still her best friend.

Lyndsey clapped her hands. "And we can end it hot tubbing at my house like the old days."

"I think it's time we go. Sounds like you have a busy day tomorrow," Andy said with a sneer on his drunken face.

"You're more than welcome to spend the day on the lake with us, Andy. You're always invited," Lyndsey said.

"I'm not going to get in the way of your girl time. It was great hanging out with you ladies tonight. I need to get our tab."

He went up to the bar.

"I'm sorry. I hope we didn't make him feel left out that we're having a girls' day. That was so rude of me," Lyndsey said.

She put her hand on Lyndsey's arm. "Not at all. I'd love a girls' day. He has his guy things. It's our day. How often do we get the opportunity to spend this much time together?"

"So true."

Andy came back, his face blotched and scowling. He took her arm and dragged her outside.

She pulled free. "What's going on, Andy? I didn't get to say goodbye to my friends. That was so rude. What's your problem, anyway?"

He gave her a cold-eyed stare. "Your friend, Ethan. He paid our damn bill."

Why was that a bad thing? "What a jerk? Paying the bill for all our friends makes him a bad person? I don't understand what you're getting at."

"I can pay our bill, Kat. He doesn't need to pay for us."

He was making way too big of a deal about this. It was a kind gesture.

"Who cares? Just say thank you. It's no big deal," she said, waving him off.

"No big deal? Don't you see he wants to get into your pants? Wake up, Kat!" He bellowed.

"Well, if he's paying for your dinner, I guess he wants to get in your pants, too."

"Very funny. You act like it's no big deal, but you were snuggling with him a little too closely on the couch the other day. Then you went and saw him and passed out, and then tonight you followed him outside when he left to take a phone call. Don't you think I should be upset about that? Do you think I'm blind?"

"Andy, I'm sorry if it looks that way. I don't know how that keeps happening, but I promise you, I don't mean to. We just have a lot of unresolved issues to deal with."

He ran his fingers through his hair, then down his face. "This isn't working."

Did she hear him right?

"What isn't working?"

"Us. You have some things you need to deal with. Before your mom died, I had a ring picked out for you. I was going to propose and now, just days later, it's as if I don't know you at all."

Her face fell. "You were going to propose?"

"Yes. I love you, Kat, but I don't want to be with you if you aren't all in. I'm heading back to the cities to give you some time to wrap this up. If you still want to be with me in a week, then we'll talk, but you need to pull yourself out of ...whatever this is. Grief maybe? I'm not sure."

Her face flicked upward. "You're leaving me here and hoping I resolve my issues so we go back to our old lives? Do you really think that's the best way to handle this?"

He let out a frustrated moan. "Kat, I don't know. All I know is you're not the woman I fell in love with, and I won't stay here and watch you flirt with your former boyfriend. I'm not that guy. Don't make me be that guy."

"Fine. Just go."

He leaned in and kissed her forehead. "I love you, Kat, but you need to figure out what you want. I'm sick of watching the two of you flirt and I know if I stay, I'll beat the crap out of him and he's not worth it. Dumb city guy."

"You do realize you're from a big city too, right?" She said, under her breath.

"Nowhere near as big as New York."

He had a point.

"I can't let you drive, Andy. You're drunk," she said gently. She didn't want to make him more angry than he already was but she didn't want him driving that far when he had been drinking all night.

"I'm not drunk."

"I'm serious. You could kill someone. Stay in one of the guest rooms, just please do't be stupid," she pleaded.

"I'm not going to kill someone. I'm fine. If I struggle to drive, I'll pull over and sleep in my truck."

He got into his truck before she had a chance to stop him and drove away. As his headlights disappeared down highway five she realized he was her ride home.

She walked into Bimbo's. Her friends shot her confused glances.

"What are you doing back?" Maddy asked.

Lyndsey stepped closer and squeezed Kat's arm. "Where is Andy? Everything okay?"

She crossed her arms. "Andy and I got into a fight. He's heading back to the cities, I guess."

Ethan's face fell. He was sure this was his fault. She could see it on his face.

"What happened?" Lyndsey stood up. "He left because I was talking about girls' day tomorrow, didn't he? I knew I put my foot in my mouth right after I said it. I'm sorry, Kat."

"No, it's not your fault. I don't know what's wrong with him but leaving was his choice. I just want to go home and get some sleep."

"I'll give you a ride," Lyndsey said.

"I'd come with you, but someone needs to drive these boys home. I think they've had too many shots" Maddy laughed and looked at Brad, who was currently slamming his beer.

"That's probably a good choice," Lyndsey said. "Let's go."

Kat glanced at Ethan with a small smile. "Thanks for dinner, Ethan."

"Anytime. I'm sorry. About everything."

"Don't be. This isn't on you, really. It was bound to happen."

He nodded, but his face still reflected guilt.

"I just need to sleep. See you tomorrow?"

His face brightened. "Definitely."

Eighteen

Ethan

Ethan helped Kevin lift the top of Lyndsey's hot tub. "This is one sweet hot tub. It's huge."

Kevin nodded. "Not as big as my parent's."

Ethan nodded. "Very true. Victoria used to beg me to take her to our hot tubbing parties at your house, but I always said no. She'd get so mad at me."

"Speaking of your sister, have you heard anything about Victoria and Troy moving here?"

Ethan got in the hot tub and sat down. "I'm not sure when, but they definitely are."

"I never thought they'd settle down in one place. They love traveling," Kevin said, following him in.

Ethan nodded. I wonder what the real reason is. My sister said Troy got a job here, but it still makes little sense why they'd change their whole life."

"The only thing that makes sense is if they're having a baby or something."

"I agree. That makes sense. Maybe they're waiting to tell us all when they get here. I never expected my sister to have kids, but good for them."

Kevin turned on the jets. "It's about time we all lived in the same place for once. You better not go back to New York now."

"I don't plan on leaving Side Lake anytime soon," Ethan said.

"You really enjoy living here, don't you? You think you'll stay? Find a place here or something? From what my brother tells me, you aren't hard up for money. What exactly is it you do? Troy said Victoria won't tell him. Is it some kind of secret?"

Ethan hated being so secretive, especially with one of his best and oldest friends. Why did everyone care so much about what he did for a living? Did it define a person's importance? If they found out he was a bestselling author, his relationships with his friends might change. He knew it would come out eventually, so he had to be honest.

"You never had a problem keeping a secret, so I'll tell you if you really want to know."

"Yes. Wait, let me guess. Are you FBI? CIA?" He made finger guns at him and laughed. "Are you a secret spy or something? Nah, I'd probably know. I can usually smell a cop from a mile away."

Ethan laughed. "I'm definitely not a cop."

Kevin climbed into the hot tub and sat across from Ethan and turned on the jets.

The water was nice and warm. His muscles ached from all the kayaking and paddle boarding he'd been doing lately.

"Spit it out. Don't leave a brother hanging."

"Okay. You won't tell anyone?"

"I absolutely will not let it leave this hot tub," Kevin said, crossing his chest with his hand.

"I'm an author."

Kevin stared at him and then started laughing. "No, seriously, what do you do?"

He shook his head and took a sip of his cold beer as he waited for Kevin to stop laughing and calm down. "Are you done?"

Kevin wiped his eyes.

"I can't help it. I can't stop laughing. Why the hell is that a secret? You can't be telling me the truth."

"I really am an author."

"And why is that such a secret? It's not like you're famous and you can't make much money off that. Very few do. There are a billion writers, let alone books out there."

Ethan shook his head and exhaled. "I don't write by my name. I write by the name of a woman. Do you know who Elizabeth Conrad is?"

Kevin's eyes widened. "Elizabeth Conrad? Like the New York Times bestselling author Elizabeth Conrad? No way. You're pulling my leg."

He nodded. This was why he told no one.

"No shit, dude. Why wouldn't you want to claim that? That's mind blowing. Romance or not, you have my respect."

He slouched down in the hot tub and looked up at the sky. "I don't know. My publicist wants me to reveal myself, but I'm happy with my life the way it is. I've been writing under a pen name for the past ten years. I don't want all the scrutiny that comes with fame. I don't want people to know me as a famous author. I enjoy living a quiet life, you know?"

"You're talking to a deputy here. I get you don't want to

be in the public eye, but man, that's huge. How am I going to be able to keep that from my wife?"

"You promised. Just wait to tell her until I decide whether to reveal myself."

"This Zoey you were talking to tonight. Is that your girlfriend?"

"No, my agent. I just finished another book, well, the rough draft anyway, and the publisher only wants it if I do a book tour, which means I need to show my face. Zoey is also negotiating a movie. What's the point of having a pen name if I have to tell everyone my real name?"

Kevin groaned. "Because it's a huge deal. You're famous. Own that. What are you scared of?"

What was he scared of? "I don't know. I'll think about it."

"Please do. This secret will kill me." Kevin shook his head. "You've dropped a lot of secrets on me over the last few days. Anything else you need to share? This is as good a time as any."

"Well, since you are asking—"

He held out a stiff arm. "Nope, don't tell me. Please, don't tell me. I don't want to know. My head is already full. Stop hiding yourself, man. These secrets will eat at you. And me."

The door creaked open behind them and Brad joined them. Ethan leaned over so only Kevin could hear. "Kat not only had the baby, but we know who our daughter is. Where she is."

Kevin's eyes opened wide. "No shit. Damn it, Ethan, I told you not to tell me."

"What's all this whispering about?" Brad asked. "You two are acting like high school girls."

Kevin looked offended and said, "We were just complimenting your tight blue shorts with that stripe. You look like a swimmer from the seventies or something. Whose are those? Your dad's old swim trunks from high school?"

"Yes, actually. It's all my dad had in the dresser downstairs, and I didn't want to run home for trunks," he said confidently. "You're just jealous because I look so good in them."

Brad walked to the hot tub with his head held high and chest puffed out. If he had Brad's confidence and carefree personality, he never would have written under a pen name and he'd be claiming his title. But he had nothing to prove to the world. He wanted to write undisturbed. Why was that such a problem? He liked everything the way it was. Less pressure.

"Where's the wife?" Kevin asked.

"I put David to bed at Lyndsey's house so Maddy could go over to Kat's." He pointed to a box on the table. "That noisy thing is the monitor." "Kat and Lyndsey are spending the night together. You know what that means."

"Strippers and beer?" Kevin said in a deep voice.

"Strippers and beer," Brad said, knocking beer bottles with him.

"In all seriousness, though, Ethan, who's this Zoey who called you tonight? Is she your new fling?"

Here we go again. "No, just a co-worker. Nothing's going on between us. It's a work thing."

Brad sat up straight in the hot tub. "There better not be," he said with a sound of warning in his voice. "Lyndsey is convinced you and Kat will end up together. And Lyndsey wants her best friend to move back, so don't screw it up."

"Nothing's going on. Trust me. Your sister has nothing to worry about."

"Alright, man. What about you? Are you sticking around for a while or what?"

"I'm not sure how long right now. I rented the cabin at Pine Beach for the rest of the year, but I'm not sure if I'm staying or not."

"What about your job? Let me guess, you can work remote." He made air quotes with his fingers. "Everyone works remote now since all the COVID stuff happened. What happened to men getting in a car and going to work to do some real physical labor?"

"We've all gone soft, Brad. That's what happened," Kevin said with a laugh.

He never had to go to work. He wrote from the convenience of his apartment, or wherever he felt like writing, way before COVID. That was a perk of his career, along with writer's block and back pain.

"So true. I'd love to see police officers doing remote work."

All three of them laughed.

Brad took a long drink of his beer. "Yeah, how would that work?"

Kevin leaned back. "It would never work. What trouble do you think the women are getting into?"

Brad put his beer in the cup holder of the hot tub. "Who knows? Probably dissing Kat's boyfriend. I don't mind the guy, but I can't believe he just walked out and drove drunk. He was taking all those shots earlier. You must have really intimidated him, huh, Ethan?"

"I hardly said two words to the guy. I think he's annoyed that Kat and I used to be a thing. He's different. It's probably for the best she got rid of the guy."

"Hello."

Ethan heard a voice from behind, and he gulped.

"I hope you don't mind me crashing your little party. I was hoping to have a chat with Lyndsey. Kat said she lived across the street but no one answered the door," Andy said.

Kevin stood up, his eyes challenging him.

Andy waved at him. "Oh, sit down. I was only here to talk to her about what was going on with Kat."

Kevin sat down, but still had a guarded look in his eyes.

"But since this dip shit is here, I'd rather have a little chat with him," Andy said. He looked in Ethan's direction, cracking his knuckles, his tone deepening.

Ethan was not the least bit threatened by him, but he just stared blankly at him.

"I thought you were going home," Kevin said, as if reading Ethan's mind. "Back to the Cities."

"Yeah, well, I didn't want to leave her alone with this guy," he said, pointing at Ethan. "And I had a little too much to drink, so I thought I'd take care of some business before I left."

Ethan glared at him. "Did you really come here just to be a dick?"

The words slipped out of his mouth without thinking, thanks to drinking a few too many beers himself.

Andy ignored Ethan's words. "Stay away from my girl. I'm not sure what your game is, but I will win and you'll lose. Mark my words."

Ethan snickered. "Is this guy a joke?"

Kevin and Brad shrugged.

"This is entertaining. Want a beer?" Brad said, throwing one to Andy.

Ethan took a drink and spit some of his beer out on the ground in reaction to his friend offering his enemy a drink.

Andy caught the bottle, twisted the cap off and threw the tab over his shoulder like a tough guy. "Don't mind if I do."

Brad thought this was funny and was egging Andy on.

"Now that we got this all out, I want you to understand I know what you're doing with Kat and it will not work."

He clenched his jaw and resisted the temptation to punch

this joke of a guy right between the eyes. "What exactly am I doing?"

"Using the good old days to win her back. I know the two of you have a child out there but—"

Brad spit a full mouth of beer into the hot tub. "A child? Huh! Did you hear that, Kev? Like that's even possible. It's the dumbest thing I ever heard. Where did you get your information, anyway?"

Kevin pounded his fist into his hand. "You come over here, uninvited, and start spilling someone else's secrets? Have some respect. This is none of your business and not your story to tell."

"Wait a minute," Brad said, sticking his hand out. "You and Kat have a child, and she was pregnant as a teenager? Does Lyndsey know? My mind is blown."

"I don't believe she knows," Kevin said.

"You knew and you don't know if your woman knows? Are you seriously keeping this from her?"

"This is Ethan's mess. He got me involved now, but in my defense I told him I didn't want to know, but he just keeps telling me shit," he said with a heavy sigh. "Lyndsey is best friends with Kat. It's possible she was sworn to secrecy as I have been."

"If you and Kat had a child, where the hell is it?"

"In Side Lake," Andy said. "But I'm going to find her, so Kat will be grateful and come running back to me."

"And what makes you think she's in Side Lake?"

"I know she is because I read this." He held up a book.

Brad's mouth dropped open. "What is that?"

Kevin got to his feet. "Give that back. You can't have that."

"No chance," Andy said with a laugh. "It's her mother's diary. Kat was struggling to read it so she asked me if I would read it for her and let her know what it said. Her mom admitted she found a worthy couple in Side Lake and had the rights signed over to them right after the baby was born.

"You jerk. I know she'd never give that journal to you," Ethan said through clenched teeth. If she wanted someone to read the journal, Andy was the last person she would ask.

"But who? Who is her daughter? I wonder if it's someone I know. Do you know the parent's names? Does it say anything at all?" Brad asked, getting all worked up.

"I don't know for sure, but I'm on a mission to find out. I doubt she wants Ethan to know since he was the reason she gave the baby away, right Ethan? I don't blame her. You don't exactly give off dad vibes. You seem more into doing push-ups. Am I right?"

Andy's cocky expression tested his self-control.

"Go home 6-1-2er. We don't want you here. You've over-stayed your welcome. Give me back my beer," Brad said.

"Really? 6-1-2er? My area code? You realize Kat has a 6-1-2 area code from the cities too, right?"

"I'm not sure why you're here," Kevin said. "Actually, I do know. You feel threatened by Ethan, right?"

Kevin climbed out of the hot tub with his chest puffed out. He transformed into a sheriff as if someone flicked a switch. He was intimidating and strong, and luckily, on Ethan's side.

"I just want to talk, wow. Seems like Ethan needs you guys to fight his battles for him. No wonder Kat ran as far as she could to get away from you and never wanted to return. She told me you ruined her life."

Ethan had enough. He got out of the hot tub and looked back at his friends. "I got this."

They both backed down.

He grabbed a towel from the railing and wrapped it around his waist.

Ethan led Andy away from the guys. "Tell me why you're really here."

"I want you to know I'm not going anywhere. Kat is mine, and you had your chance with her. You're not much of a man. You could have found her years ago, but you didn't care enough."

Was that true? Did he give up too easily? Could he have tried harder? He was here now, and he would fight for Kat. This guy would never treat her right. "What did you think you'd accomplish by coming here?"

"I'll show you," Andy said.

He ran into the side mirror of his truck. He fell on the sidewalk and screamed in pain. Once he finally stood up, his right eye was red and swollen.

"I can't believe you punched me. Kat will never forgive you for this," Andy said with a wink. "Just try to deny it. You're messing with the wrong guy."

"She'll never believe you."

"Oh, won't she? We'll see about that."

Nineteen

Kat

Lyndsey walked Kat inside and rifled through her cupboards.

Kat sat on the kitchen counter. "What are you looking for?"

"Marshmallows and wine. I brought graham crackers and chocolate. We'll go outside and start a fire. Maddy will be here soon, and we'll chat and have a girl's night. I told her to grab some clothes for me to sleep in and my overnight bag. In the morning we'll keep sorting and then go boating in the afternoon. How does that sound?"

Kat smiled and tears formed in her eyes. She blinked them away.

"I forgot what it was like to have good friends."

"Just wait until you meet Whitney. She's a schoolteacher here in Hibbing and a good friend of Maddy's. She's meeting up with us tomorrow afternoon."

"I can't wait to meet her."

141

Lyndsey gathered all the s'more stuff and a bottle of wine. They opened the bottle, grabbed three glasses, and headed out the door. They sat everything down on the deck and Lyndsey arranged the wood in the firepit in a teepee fashion.

"Crap. I don't have a lighter," Kat said. "Let me run inside."

Lyndsey pulled one out of her pocket. "I got you beat."

"Nice. Thank you."

Lyndsey poked at the fire with a metal pole.

"Can I ask you a question?"

"Anything."

"I never directly asked you because I thought you would tell me when you were ready, but you still haven't so I need to ask you," Lyndsey rambled.

She knew what was coming. Time to fess up.

"What was in that note you had me give Ethan the day you left?"

"I'm sorry I never told you. You're right, it wasn't easy, and I was scared. Time passed and it was easier pushing it all in the back of my mind than telling you the truth."

"You don't have to tell me if you don't want to, I just want you to know whatever it is, I won't judge. But I've come up with so many explanations over the years, but I never really knew for sure."

It was so hard to tell her after hiding it all these years. She finally said, "I had you bring Ethan that note because I was pregnant and ending things. I asked him to sign paperwork to give up the baby."

Lyndsey was silent, waiting for Kat to continue.

"I knew I wasn't ready to have a child and my mom didn't give me much of a choice either. That's why she made me move in with my aunt. At first, I thought I was having an abortion, but so many people want babies and can't have them, like my aunt."

Lyndsey reached over and took her hand, squeezing it lightly.

"I decided to give my baby up for adoption and my mom handled everything. I guess in the back of my mind I always blamed my mom. I was upset she didn't tell me who was adopting my baby. She didn't want anyone in Side Lake to know or her perfect image would be destroyed. That hurt. And it hurt that she sent me away, although I'm grateful she found the baby a good home."

"Have you and Ethan spoken about it since you've been home?"

"Yes."

How much should she tell Lyndsey? She wanted to blurt out that they found their daughter, that her daughter was the daughter of Lyndsey's employer, but she also knew that wasn't fair to Ethan or their daughter's adopted parents. She needed to tell them first and see how they reacted before she told her best friend everything.

"And what did he say? You haven't talked since you wrote that letter, right?"

"No, not until my mother's funeral, but we've been spending a lot of time together. It started off pretty nasty, as you saw. We still give each other crap sometimes, but I don't hate him anymore."

Lyndsey laughed. "That's good. I can't believe you had a child and never told me. Was it a boy or a girl? I want to know everything."

"A girl."

"A girl? What did you name her? Did you get to name her? I have so many questions, "Lyndsey said," her eyes sparkled as she spoke. "This is just so mind blowing. I always had my suspicions, but I never expected them to be true."

"I'm sorry I hid it from you. I didn't get to name her or even hold her."

"Don't be sorry. I'm the one who should be sorry for letting you carry this on your own. You didn't even get to hold her? That's horrible."

Lyndsey did not know the worst of it.

"Will you try to find her?"

She searched for a way around answering that question.

"Well, the thing is my mom had this journal that she started when she was pregnant with me."

"No way! Did you read it?"

"I started to, and I actually felt like I was understanding why she was the way she was. I hoped to find answers about my biological daughter in there and I was slowly reading it. But then ..."

"But then?"

"But then the journal went missing. I'm not sure what I did with it. I was certain I put it in a box in the living room after I caught Andy trying to read it, but then it disappeared into thin air."

"He was reading it? That's not okay. Do you think he found it and took it?"

She shook her head. Would Andy do that? Did she really know him at all? Those entries were for her to read, not someone else. They were personal and even though she had despised her mother, she despised her a little less now that she was getting to know her through her diary. But no one else had the right to read it.

"Ugh. I don't know. If he did, I am going to be pissed." She tried to call him, but her call went right to voicemail.

"Damn it, his phone is off.'

"He's probably in a dead spot. Try calling him again a little later. Now, tell me how you are going to find your daughter?"

"First, I'll finish reading my mom's diary, if I can find it. I believe the answers are in there. The answers to who my father is and the answers to so many questions I have about my mom. She just cut me off. Who does that to their daughter?"

Lyndsey shook her head.

"Hey ladies!" Maddy called out to them. "Is that a wine bottle I see? I'm so excited!"

Maddy carried a duffel bag over each shoulder as she made her way toward them. "I'm dying for some chocolate." She looked from Lyndsey to her and back to Lyndsey. "What did I miss? You two look so serious. Is everything okay?"

We both nodded.

"Kat found her mom's journal and put it in a box and now it's missing."

"Missing? Oh, no. Do you think you misplaced it?"

"I'm not sure."

"So, how's David?" Kat said to change the subject. "Did he go to bed okay?"

"Yeah. I left him with the boys at Lyndsey's house. They were getting ready to jump in the hot tub when I left. Brad volunteered to put David to bed so I could hang out with you guys."

Her phone buzzed. "This is really weird, but I just got a text from Brad that Andy showed up at Lyndsey's house after I left."

"Are you serious? I hope he didn't go there to start trouble. What was I thinking being in a relationship with him for so long?" Her heart thumped in her chest. "He better not have started more trouble with Ethan. He needed to get over it. It was his decision to break up with her. "He better not show up here next."

Lyndsey rubbed her eyebrow. "Do you think we should sneak over there and see if he left yet?"

Maddy stuffed her hands in her jacket pocket. "I'm not sure I want to be caught in the middle of that. The boys can handle him. This is our night."

"You're right," Kat said. "They can handle Andy. They don't need us."

"Cheers to that."

They all clinked glasses.

"Now, let's have some wine and s'mores," Kat said with a laugh. "Forget about the boys for one night."

"Deal," Lyndsey and Maddy said in unison. They picked up their glasses and clinked them again. She could get used to having good friends in her life. A part of her never wanted to leave this place, and the other part was telling her to run as far and fast as she could.

Twenty

Ethan

Thirty minutes later the police arrived at Lyndsey's house and Ethan was in handcuffs.

"I didn't hit him. He ran into his car mirror."

"You really expect us to believe that?" the deputy said.

He would have a hard time believing it if someone told him that story, too. He was screwed.

"Finney, what are you doing here?" the deputy said, as Kevin walked up to them.

"This is my girlfriend's house."

"Tracey?"

He shook his head. "Very funny. No, Lyndsey."

"Nice place. You didn't happen to see what happened out here did you?"

"This guy," he said pointing at Andy. "Comes over here uninvited, ready to pick a fight. I didn't see what happened, but he came here ready to brawl."

"I'm sorry, man, but we have to take your guy into custody."

"I know." Kevin looked at Ethan and back to the officer. "Can I walk him to your car?"

"Go ahead, I need to get a statement from the victim, anyway."

Ethan was cuffed and read his rights. His legs shook, and he worried they would collapse beneath him. How did he get here? He had never been in trouble with the law in his life.

Kevin grabbed his upper arm gently and led him to the patrol car.

"What the hell happened? You took the guy around the corner and beat the crap out of him? I didn't know you had it in you."

"No. I didn't touch him. I told him to leave, and he got upset and ran full speed into his side mirror."

Kevin scrunched up his face and pinched his nose, deep in thought. "Okay, I'll talk to the deputy and get him to take a look at the mirror. If your story is accurate, there has to be some damage. But Ethan, his nose won't stop bleeding, and his eyes are swollen. If you don't have any proof, this could be a problem. I'll see what I can do, okay?" He put him in the back of the patrol car, shut the door, and walked away.

It felt like forever before the officer returned to the car. He got into the front seat and shut the door.

"I still have to take you in because now he's insisting you threw him into the mirror."

Ethan sighed. "How can he go from saying that I punched him to I pushed him into his car mirror?"

"If he did this to himself, he's an idiot. The truth will come out eventually, it usually does with guys like that. Don't worry, you'll be seen in front of a judge within seventy-two hours of your arrest. Get a lawyer and you can fight this. Okay?"

He nodded. Kevin was a deputy but even he could not get him out of this mess.

He was angry and scared to be put into a jail cell. What would it look like? Would he have to share it with someone or multiple people?

They pulled up at the sally port in front of the jail and the garage door opened after a few words were exchanged into the speaker. Once the garage door closed behind them, the officer escorted him into the cold, dark jail.

He sat down in front of the deputy and waited for the jailer to do his rounds. He made Ethan feel a lot less nervous joking with him and telling him funny Kevin stories. It helped that the deputy knew he and Kevin were good friends and that Kevin's brother Troy married his sister. The deputy even told him he had been at the wedding because he knew Troy from high school.

Once the other deputy was done making his rounds, she patted him down.

"Be easy on this guy. He has no criminal history, and he's a good friend of Finney's."

The jailer did not look amused.

The deputy stood by the counter as Ethan answered questions for the jailer. It started off with basic questions and then suicidal questions. Once he was done, he asked, "If I would have said yes, what would you have to do? Take me to the hospital?"

"You'd be on suicide watch and it's no fun. Now I need you to wash your hands and use the restroom, and we'll begin the fingerprint process."

He washed his hands as directed. Plastic shower shoes replaced his own shoes. Fingerprints seemed to take forever, but they were not done by dipping his hands in ink like he expected. They were done on the computer. Next, he stood in front of the wall for a picture.

The entire process was embarrassing. Should he smile or cry?

"Go ahead and pick out a book in that rack over there," the deputy instructed.

The first book he laid eyes on was his own book. How ironic.

She was kind and seemed to do her job without judgment. For that, he was grateful. She escorted him to a cell. "In you go."

Cement walls surrounded his cell and had a solid metal door that echoed when shut. The room had a table, a hard bed with blankets, and a toilet and sink. The camera was aimed right at him.

She gave him his toiletries and locked him in before leaving.

He lay on the bed, the room chilly and the smell of bleach filling his nostrils. When he coughed, it echoed off the walls. He was alone.

The deputy was the only person he saw as she did her rounds every hour. A buzzer that went off now and then scared the crap out of him every time it went off. Just when he finally fell asleep, a key in the door woke him. The guard peeked through the window at him and swiped something by the door.

Another deputy brought him a plate of food in the morning.

"If you plan on getting your own attorney, I highly recommend Dennis Carlton. He's the best." He handed him a card through the cell.

"Thanks. Why are you giving me this?"

"As a favor to Deputy Finney. He's a good guy."

Ethan nodded, and the deputy nodded back and walked away.

The deputy later brought him his written charges and his

rights and a ton of other paperwork. "We're waiting for the county attorney to charge you." He shrugged. "You may even be seen this morning if they do it fast enough."

All he could think about was what a terrible person Andy was to lie. Kat would never believe he was innocent, just like the guys. He did nothing wrong but felt like a criminal. He did not deserve this. He didn't do it, but how was he going to prove it?

Two deputies came in to get him for his arraignment at approximately eleven thirty. He looked down at the paint on his gray t-shirt. What would the judge think?

He sat down in front of the camera and listened while the judge spoke with another guy on the screen. The guy argued and said something about being a sovereign citizen. Was this a joke? People really did that?

He was surprised at the calmness the judge displayed. The judge told the guy he was being held without bail and set a court date. Ethan was next.

"State your name for the record and give us your address and phone number, please."

He did as directed.

"Do you understand what you are being charged with? Not that you agree with it, but do you understand what you are being charged with?"

"Yes, sir." He was being charged with misdemeanor assault.

"And do you understand your rights?"

"Yes, sir."

"Okay, I'm ordering a restraining order so you can not have any contact with the alleged victim, and that includes through a third party. Do you understand that?"

He never wanted to talk to or see that jerk again anyway, so it would not be a problem. "Yes, sir," he repolied.

"It looks like you don't qualify for a public defender. Do you wish to hire a lawyer yourself?"

"Yes, Your Honor."

No way was he going to get charged without a lawyer to defend him.

"Okay, I'm releasing you on pre-trial release. Probation will meet with you today to sign your conditions. Your bail is set at $20,000. Next court date is..."

Ethan stopped listening. Twenty thousand dollars? How was he going to come up with that on his own without letting his agent know what it was for?"

He pled not guilty and hoped he did the right thing. Within an hour of returning to his cell he had met with a probation officer, gone over his conditions, and was being released on probation.

"Your bail was paid so you don't need to check in with probation. You may want to notify them though," the deputy said. "Wouldn't want them to put out a warrant if they think you skipped out on checking in."

The deputy showed no emotion when he looked at Ethan or talked to him. He felt a lot more like a criminal in this guy's presence. He was given back his belongings and was out the door within twenty-four hours of his arrest. What was the point of that?

Kevin was waiting for him outside.

"Andy called Kat and told her you punched him."

"But I didn't. I swear to you."

He nodded, crossing his arms. "Oh, I know. I had a little talk with him, and he admitted everything. Said he's going to the police and let them know what happened, get the charges and restraining order dropped. I'm really sorry you had to deal with this."

Ethan blinked. "You believed me? Is that why you talked to him?"

"Of course I believed you. Look at your hands."

He examined his hand closely, trying to understand what Kevin meant.

"You don't have a mark on you. If you were in a fight with this guy, I doubt you fought back or there would be evidence on you."

That was true. Why hadn't he thought of that?

He couldn't wait to be back in his cabin and have a hot shower and go to bed. But sleep eluded him that night. He tossed and turned, memories of being in that tiny cell haunting him. But most of all, he thought about Kat and whether she believed him.

Andy went way too far this time. If he could do something like this, what would he do to Kat? Would he follow through and make sure the charges got dropped or would he be a coward and lie once again? He did not want to think about it.

Twenty-One

Kat

When Kevin told her Ethan had been arrested for punching Andy, she was livid. Did she know him at all? Although her first thought was that Andy probably had it coming to him. But to punch Andy in the face and shatter his nose was horrid. She was falling for Ethan and in an instant it all disappeared. He was no longer the man she knew.

Even though Kevin did not think Ethan did it, she could tell in his voice he was trying to convince himself that Ethan was innocent. "I asked Ethan if he hit Andy and either he's a really good liar or he was being honest," he said at last.

She hung up the phone, and Lyndsey was by her side. "Was that Kevin? What happened?"

"Ethan punched Andy and shattered his nose, but Ethan insists it didn't happen that way. He says Andy ran into the side mirror on his car on purpose to make it look like he hit him."

Lyndsey pulled out her phone.

"What are you doing?"

"My dad has trail cameras in the driveway. I can look it up on my phone."

Lyndsey pulled the video up and they watched as Andy and Ethan yelled at each other, and then just like Ethan said, Andy ran full force into his side mirror. He said something to Ethan, then smiled as the blood ran down his face. He even spit out a tooth.

Kat shuddered when she watched him spit the tooth out and smile with blood in his teeth. So disgusting and evil. To think she almost married that guy.

Kat screamed at the camera. "That jerk! He set Ethan up and had him arrested for that? I'm calling Kevin right now."

Within the hour, Kevin was able to send the video to the county attorney and Ethan's charges were dropped.

Kevin told her he paid Ethan's bail to have him released from jail. He said Ethan walked out of jail with puffy eyes and dark circles around them. Her heart hurt at the thought. Her ex-boyfriend did that to Ethan and it was all her fault. And she actually believed Andy when he called and told her Ethan punched him. She was so naïve.

She hurried to his cabin to see him. "I'm so sorry, Ethan."

His face lit up when he saw her. She wrapped her arms around his shoulders. "I can't believe Andy actually did that to himself."

"How—how do you know? How'd you find out I wasn't lying?"

"Lyndsey's dad had a trail cam set up in his driveway to watch for deer. We have the whole thing on video."

He shook his head, his expression upset and confused. "You have to really despise someone to do that to yourself."

"He was so jealous and obviously desperate because he felt like you were competition. It's my fault for letting him come here, and for introducing you," she said, looking away.

He took her hand and held it to his chest. His heart was beating fast. She shivered beneath his touch.

"It's not your fault."

"But I should have—"

"There was nothing you could have done. You couldn't have known. Look at me." He tilted her chin up until their eyes met. "It's not your fault, and I don't want to hear another word about it."

She nodded, blinking back the tears.

"Let's get out of here, okay? Why don't we get some loaded hash browns at the Howard Court in Hibbing?"

From the outside, the Howard Court looked like any other building in town. But once they walked inside, it was clean and inviting with blue carpet and offices on both sides. A beautiful stairwell split the building in half.

Kat looked around. "How did I not know about this place?"

She followed him down the hall to a little cafe. The smell of breakfast and coffee filled the air, and she breathed in deeply. Her stomach growled.

"Order whatever toppings you'd like. You do like loaded hash browns, correct?"

"I love hash browns, so yes."

Ethan cleared his throat. "I'll have your loaded hash

browns with pepper jack cheese, sausage and green peppers with a side of English muffin toast and a coffee."

The woman shot her a friendly smile. "And for you, dear?"

"I'll have the loaded hash browns with a coffee, and American cheese, bacon, mushrooms, and a side of pancakes."

They paid and took a seat at the only open table.

"This place is really popular, huh?" She looked around her at all the tables of people.

He gave her a grin that took her breath away. "You'll see why once you taste the hash browns."

He was a naturally handsome man with broad shoulders and a killer grin. Confident but not cocky, he took good care of himself and it showed in his toned body. She stared at his arms as they peeked out from beneath his t-shirt. The guy had not showered and was wearing the same shirt after spending a night in jail and he never looked better.

She mentally shook her head out of the gutter. She just got out of a relationship. Well, kind of got out of a relationship. The image of Andy running into that truck and then smiling back at Ethan made her stomach turn. How could he do that and not feel guilty?

"Was it horrible?" She finally said. "Jail that is?"

He clenched his jaw and held his coffee cup in both hands.

"It was fine. Not a place I plan on visiting again any time soon though."

She smiled at him, and he grinned back, his eyes locking with hers.

"We have had little time to talk, just the two of us. I want to hear what you've been up to."

"Well, I work for child protection down in Hennepin County. It's a tough job, but some days I feel like I make kids' lives a little less horrible when they've had no one they could trust not to hurt them. I help keep them safe and that means everything to me. Lyndsey hated working in child protection, but I don't mind it. It's not that bad. It's stressful but when I get that call to respond to a child in imminent danger, it gets my blood flowing. I love the rush, and I thrive on beating the danger." She looked up at him to see if he was bored. "I'm one-of-a-kind, I know. I love how intense it is sometimes, and I love putting intimidating child beaters in their place. I also really love working with and helping victims. I'm a big advocate for Advocates For Family Peace. Okay, I'm rambling."

"No need to apologize. I love the way you look when you're passionate about something. I remember you being that way when we were teenagers. You're amazing, you know that? I've never met anyone like you, trust me, I've looked."

Her face grew hot, but she did not want him to see her looking vulnerable. "Thank you." That was the sweetest thing he'd ever said to her, and she felt the meaning behind his words.

"So, you told me you write books, but I want to hear more about them. Have you been published? Do you make any money? I have a friend of a friend who signed a three-book deal and got fifty grand and her editor quit after the first book was published. She got a new editor and a year later they ended up not wanting the other two books and she had to pay back most of the advance. Lost her house and everything."

He nodded. "Yeah, that stuff happens all too often with big publishing companies, especially if you have a book that flops."

"So why don't people go with smaller publishing companies then?"

"I don't know. There's always a risk, no matter which direction you go. You have to love what you do. I never went into it for the money. Smaller publishing companies are great, but you won't get the same payout and you worry about them going under. It's hard for authors and publishers to keep afloat with all the books out there today. People haven't stopped reading books, but they have more options now with e-readers and audiobooks. I never started writing to be rich, I did it because I wasn't me if I wasn't writing."

"I like that."

A waitress brought the food to their table. "Here you go. Do you need anything else?"

They both shook their heads.

"This looks great, thank you," Ethan said.

"Wow, that's a lot of hash browns," she said, then she took a bite. "Oh my. These are the best hash browns I've ever tasted."

He smiled. "Told you so."

"So, back to writing. By writing a book you aren't instantly rich?"

"No. So many people think that but no. Publishers don't put a lot of money into marketing so we have to market our books for ourselves, and it isn't as easy as it seems. It's also really expensive."

"Do you make okay money?"

"You could say that. But my agent almost dropped me because she did not like my latest books until this one I wrote while I was here."

"That's terrible." She shook her head at the thought. "I would hate the stress of that. Did you get a new agent then?"

"No, I came back here because I knew I would find the inspiration I'd been lacking since I stopped spending my summers here. New York isn't all I thought it would be. It wasn't good for my creative mind."

"Let me get this straight, you left New York to live in the natural forests of the great north woods, huh?"

"It's the best decision I ever made. And it led me back to you." He touched her hand and she smiled.

His words made her heart flutter. Did he mean it?

"Ever since I found out our daughter lives in the same small town I grew up in, I can't help but be grateful I wasn't too stubborn to come back. I hope Emma will understand why we had to do what we did and being abandoned by her biological parents didn't leave too big a scar on her heart."

"Me too, but I keep reminding myself only she can make that decision and we owe it to Amy and Mark to give them a heads up."

"I know, you're right. We can only hope they'll be supportive."

Twenty-Two

Ethan

He skipped his run and met everyone at Lyndsey's for a day of boating like the old days. He and Kat decided they would wait and enjoy the day relaxing in the sun and boating with their friends before they talked to Emma's parents.

He was walking down Lyndsey's driveway when Zoey called.

"Hey, Zoey, what's up?"

"Ethan, I'm so glad you answered. I heard you were in jail. What the hell happened and how did you get out already?"

'What... how did you find out?'

"Ethan, haven't you looked at your phone? What am I saying? You've been in jail. You probably haven't looked at your phone. You're all over social media. Somehow the world found out who you really are, and that you were in jail for assault charges. Did you really punch a guy? I've been dealing with this all morning. You can imagine the uproar when people found out Elizabeth Conrad is actually a man."

"So is Viola Shipman and everyone loves him."

"He didn't try to hide it. There is a big difference."

Anxiety hit him like a block to the head. "What? How does everyone know who I am just because I was in jail? This is why I didn't want anyone to know who I was. Damn it." He looked around him. "Does everyone know where I am now?"

"Not that I know of. I'm trying to find that out."

"This is so bad." His hands were shaking, and he had a hard time holding his phone against his ear. "I haven't told my friends yet. I guess I can't wait any longer."

Zoey let out a loud breath. "If these are your real friends, you should probably tell them before they find out. Fast. The timing is perfect with the announcement of your new book and possible movie deal. I couldn't have planned this better myself. Well, if you hadn't been arrested it would be a lot better. Also, did you know Hibbing is Bob Dylan's home-town? Absolutely fabulous! The media will have a field day with this when it comes out that you were hiding in a northern Minnesota lake town." She was rambling which could only mean one thing, his skeletons were bringing him to the spotlight and although he liked Zoey, any publicity was good publicity for her.

"Ethan, is that you? Who are you talking to?"

Kat put her hand on his shoulder, and he turned around to stare at her.

"Listen, I have to go. Thank you for handling this." He hung up without giving Zoey a chance to answer.

He spun around and smiled at Kat. She had on a blue dress that brought out her eyes.

He wanted to tell her, but all he could think about was how beautiful she looked. Besides, they would be boating all day, and she would not be on her phone. If she didn't know who he was already, she would not find out until at least tonight. He would spend the day on the lake with his friends, enjoying his normal life before he told them the truth. Then they would hate him for keeping this secret. Wouldn't they? At least the guys already knew.

Kat's bright pink swimsuit peeked out from beneath her dress. Was she wearing a bikini or a one piece? He could not be sure, but it intrigued him. The dress hugged her curves and drew his eyes slowly down every inch of her body.

She looked down and pulled at the fabric on her dress. "What? Do I have a stain on my dress?"

"No, you look absolutely gorgeous and I can't take my eyes off you."

She blushed and pushed her hair behind her ears. "In this old thing? I've had it for years. Now, if you're done ogling me, lets hurry and catch up to everyone. They must be inside waiting for us."

The front door was locked, so they went around to the back. Everyone was by the dock, waiting for them.

"Sorry we're late," Kat said. She held on to Ethan's hand as she stepped in and then helped Kevin drop the ropes and bumpers before pushing the boat off the dock and jumping in.

The MasterCraft X star was a beautiful boat. Red and white with a tower and a black Bimini top to give them shade from the sun.

The lake was packed with boats on this hot August afternoon. They took off toward Big Sturgeon Lake, the biggest lake on the chain.

"How are the channels? Are they deep enough this year?" he said to Kevin.

"Water levels were really high at the beginning of the summer, I guess, but they're much lower now. Not enough rain this summer. We'll be careful going under the bridges so the prop doesn't hit the bottom, or we'll be in trouble."

"This is a beautiful boat. I can't believe you let Kevin drive it," he said to Lyndsey.

Lyndsey laughed. "Kevin's a pro. My parents gave me this boat with the house. They can't drive it anymore, but they wanted me to keep it. I don't mind taking it out. Are you going to wakeboard?"

He glanced at the wakeboard hanging on the rack. "What kind of wakeboard you got up there?"

"It's Brad's," Lyndsey said.

"It's a Liquid Force," Brad said, loud enough to be heard over the engine.

Ethan leaned toward Kevin so he could hear him better. "Have you gotten better on the wakeboard since the last time I saw you?"

Kevin grinned. "I still can't wakeboard, but I remember you being pretty damn good at it. Are you going to put on a show for us today?"

"It's been a while, but I'll try," Ethan said.

Brad adjusted the rearview mirror. "It's like riding a bike."

Like riding an unsteady bike and falling and hitting cement. He had some hard falls in his younger years and he got hurt many times. He could not imagine what that would feel like as an adult. "I'm not sure this old body remembers how to wakeboard anymore."

Kevin patted him on the back. "You aren't that old. I never could do it, but I'm much better at watching."

Brad pulled back on the throttle and the engine quieted so they could hear each other better. "What lake do you want to try?"

"Little Sturgeon or West Sturgeon. The waves are too rough out here. West Sturgeon is better for skiing and board-ing. The water is warm and the lake isn't too big."

"I might just have to ski later," Lyndsey said.

"You're one heck of a skier. That I do remember," Ethan said.

Lyndsey made her way to the back of the boat and opened a compartment. "We have sandwiches in the cooler and drinks, too if anyone wants one."

They all raised their hands, so she passed out sandwiches and drinks.

The sun was warm and not a cloud blemished the sky. The air was thick and wet, but when the boat was moving, it was hard to tell how hot it was. He caked on the sunscreen to protect his fair skin that seemed to burn in the shade at times.

Kat scooted closer to him on the seat so he could hear her over the loud boat. "Need me to put some on your back?"

How could he say no to her hands all over his body? "Sure. Thank you."

He felt the chill when she touched him, and he broke out in goosebumps beneath her touch. Her hands felt soft as she rubbed the sunscreen on his back with such delicate strokes. He needed a distraction and fast. "Do you still ski, Kat?"

"I haven't in years. I love skiing but I'm not amazing at it."

He nodded and put his hand over hers and rubbed it. She slid her thighs closer to him and he put his arm on the top of the seat behind her.

Lyndsey and Maddy were at the front of the boat, and Brad was chatting with Kevin. That meant they were alone, and no one was paying attention to them.

He leaned into her and put his lips to her ear. "Correct me if I'm wrong, but you're officially single now, aren't you?"

"Yes, never again with that guy. It should have been over a

long time ago. I stayed in that toxic relationship because I thought I should settle. The truth is someone long ago set the standards so high that I've struggled to find anyone even close."

The speeding boat created a strong wind that messed with her hair. He pushed hair out of her face. "Sounds like a man you never should have let go."

She turned her head and stared into his eyes. Had he offended her or didn't she catch his reference. He tried again. "I never stopped thinking about you after all these years, you know."

She ran her thumb along his strong jawline. "Oh, really? And why did it take you this long to find me then?"

"I didn't think you wanted to hear from me. I tried hard to find you, you know. I even wrote you a letter."

"I never got it."

"I figured as much. I was dumb enough to mail it to your mom's thinking she would forward it on. I never stopped trying, although I know now, I should have tried harder. I didn't want to believe you weren't coming back. I loved you and never stopped thinking about you or our baby."

"Loved me?"

The word seemed to confuse her, but he needed let her know how he felt. He leaned in and kissed her. Her lips were soft and warm and inviting. When their lips finally broke apart, he said, "That was everything I dreamed it would be."

"Did you two just kiss?" Brad said.

Lyndsey's face lit up. "It's about damn time. We all saw it coming."

The attention made him nervous, so he yelled out a sarcastic, "Did we? I don't think we did. Maybe we should do it again."

"Oh, stop," Kat said, and hit his shoulder playfully. "Why don't you show us all up with your wake boarding skills instead?"

"Okay," he said loud enough for Kevin and Brad to hear. "I'll do my best on that wakeboard but just remember I'm a bit rusty."

"Ah, you'll be fine," Kevin said.

"West Sturgeon then?"

"How about Little Sturgeon instead? It's a longer run and less traffic."

They made their way down the channel and toward Little.

The boat stopped, and Kat looked over the side of the boat at the water. "Kevin, why is the water so dark over here?"

Brad threw a life jacket at Ethan and said, "All the water run-off flows into this lake."

Ethan put on his life jacket and made his way to the swim deck. The water felt chilly on his feet. "Hey, where's the wakeboard?"

Brad passed it to him.

He put on the bindings, grabbed the end of the rope, and slid into the water. Within a moment, the chill was gone, and the water felt warm. He leaned back in the water and held onto the handle until the boat finally was far enough away to tighten the rope.

"Go."

The engine roared and brought him to his feet. He crossed the wake back and forth until he was comfortable. Now for some tricks. He squatted down, hit the wake and jumped. He almost cleared the other side of the wake, but he went flying into the water headfirst.

The engine slowed, and the boat circled around.

Brad stuck his head over the side of the boat and whistled. "That was close, man. Try to load up the rope more and let the board and the wake do the work."

Ethan nodded and grabbed onto the rope. "How fast were you going?"

Brad turned around to look at the speedometer, as if the answers were there. "Ah, about twenty, twenty-one."

"Why don't you punch it up to about twenty-three."

Brad straightened out the boat. Once the rope was tight again, Ethan called out 'go' and Brad punched it again.

Ethan set himself up, and this time when he jumped the wake, he cleared it on the other side and everyone in the boat erupted in cheers and clapping. He kept going until his thigh crashed against the water as if he hit a concrete wall instead of water.

When the boat came back around, everyone asked if he was okay and he heard the word ouch several times.

"That was a tough fall, but damn you looked good out there," Kevin said.

Kat leaned over the side of the boat. "You going again?"

"Nah, that one rang my bell. I think it's time you show me up, Brad."

Brad smirked. "Alright."

Not only did Brad clear the wake, making it look easy, he did back rolls, landing perfectly balanced without even the slightest bit of a wobble. The cheers were even louder. He was slaying it.

Ethan could watch Brad wakeboard for hours. He did four long runs before calling it quits. On one run, he almost smoked a loon.

As Brad hopped in the boat, he tried to hand the wakeboard to Kevin.

Kevin waved him off. "Nope, not for me. I may ski later, but I'm not a wake boarder. If I tried doing the things you guys did, I'd probably break something."

"Lyndsey?" Brad asked.

"Today I'm having a white claw and relaxing. I'm here for the entertainment. Another day."

"Kat?"

"Nope."

"Maddy?"

"I'm good, too."

"Well, let's have some sandwiches and go cruising then."

Brad opened the cooler in the back hatch and passed them out.

"I miss the beach days. This is awesome," Ethan said.

He also loved that Kat kept getting closer to him, her leg so close to his that their legs bumped together every time the boat hit a wave.

They slowed down through the channels and waved at the other boaters. Why did he ever leave this place? It felt so good to be home.

They went back to Lyndsey's around six to make pizzas in her wood fire grill. She made the dough, and they all took turns topping the pizzas. Kevin and Brad cooked them on the stove for everyone.

Ethan sat down next to Kat and their legs touched beneath the table. Their bodies were like magnets. The thought of jail and the incident the night before was erased from his mind and all he thought about was her lips and their kiss.

He needed to tell her about his job, but he held back. Now was not the right time. Maybe at the bonfire.

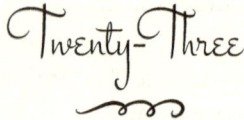

Twenty-Three

Kat

Lyndsey was once again the one to start the campfire. Kevin tried to help but Lyndsey shot him the look of death. He laughed and gave her a kiss before sitting in front of the fire with everyone else. The darkness of the night and the brightness of the bonfire blocked their view of the lake.

They sat around with White Claws and beer. The fire warmed the chilly air. In the cities, the temperature was always at least ten degrees warmer than in the north.

Kat relaxed in her chair. She belonged here, sitting around the campfire with her favorite people.

Brad grabbed another beer out of the cooler. "So, Kat, what's your plan now?"

She looked over to Brad. Everyone else was busy chatting in their own side conversations and not paying any attention to them. "Huh?"

"With everything that happened with that crazy ex of

yours, Andy, right? It seems like you and my boy Ethan are hitting it off. Are you still planning on selling your mom's house?"

"Yes."

Brad had never shown any interest in her life before. She felt awkward talking to him even though he was Lyndsey's older brother and she'd known him since she was a child. Why was he interested now?

He looked over at Lyndsey, and she turned her head to see her, too. She was busy chatting with Maddy, and they were laughing about something.

"Lyndsey has been worried about you since the day you left. This is the happiest I've seen her in such a long time. Between having you here and her relationship with Kevin, she's on top of the world. Kat, I know we aren't really close, and I was kind of a jerk when we were kids, but you belong here. I'd hate to see you sell your mom's house and then regret it."

She had the same worries. She wanted to live close to Lyndsey and all her friends. She wanted to be in Side Lake, but to live alone in that gigantic house she hated so much? That house would never be her home. Not without all the memories that came with it. The house was a giant, empty house from her childhood with no love and that's what it would always be to her.

"All I'm saying is to make sure this is what you really want." He reached over and patted her arm.

This was the soft side of Brad she had yet to see.

"Don't be in too big of a rush to leave. You belong here."

She pulled her hand away. "I appreciate you looking out for me, Brad, but I can't stay here. It's just—"

A strong voice from behind cut her off. "Hey guys, hi Kat. I've heard so much about you, and I'm sorry to hear about your mom."

Lyndsey stood up. "Kat, this is one of Maddy and my best friends, Whitney, and her husband Josh."

"Hello," they said in unison.

"Have a drink. Here you go." Kevin grabbed two beers and handed them out.

"Thanks."

"Yeah, thanks," Josh said. He followed his wife to two open chairs next to Kat. Whitney sat in the chair right next to Kat and Josh sat on the other side of his wife.

"I'm so excited to finally meet you in person. Lyndsey has told us so much about you."

"This is the woman who helped pull me out of the darkest time in my life after Ariel passed," Maddy said, her face full of emotion.

"She's the reason we ended up back together," Brad said, kissing his wife's hand.

"What do you mean?"

"Well, Brad and I got divorced, and I was so depressed for so long after the car accident. I finally went back to work and Whitney brought me back to life and helped me realize what was in front of me the whole time." She looked over at Brad, and they smiled at each other with adoration and respect on their faces.

"I was running from life for so long and Whitney helped me find myself and realize I needed to move forward and that I could use my grief to drive me." She wiped the tears streaking down her face and Kat did the same.

"That's sure a welcoming speech," Whitney said with a smile. She hugged Maddy.

Lyndsey hit Brad in the shoulder. "Hey, I helped. I beat some sense into this brother of mine."

He held his arm like she hurt him. "Hey, come on now. I never stopped trying to get her back."

· · ·

"Sure," Maddy said.

She knew there was more to the story.

"I'm not looking forward to going back to work in a few weeks, are you?" Maddy said to Whitney.

Whitney let out a loud breath. "I'm excited to meet the kids, but I hate that summer is coming to an end."

"Whitney is a teacher at Dylan Elementary. We hit it off immediately, many years ago." Maddy turned to Whitney. "Kat here is a social worker like Lyndsey was."

"In child protection?" Whitney asked.

Kat nodded.

Whitney scratched her jaw. "Oh, yikes. Lyndsey was always so stressed out when she had that job."

"I don't mind it. Then again, I've been doing it for so long it seems like my normal now."

"The turnover is bad here. If you decided to stay you could get a job in no time," Lyndsey said.

Kat was unsure how to respond. Did she want to keep working in child protection? Was there a chance she would change her mind and stay? Then she thought of Emma. Could she leave Emma if her daughter wanted them in her life?

Kevin stood and shushed the group. "Everyone here is family to Lyndsey and me, and I want you all here to witness this."

He pulled Lyndsey to her feet, holding both of her hands in between them.

"Lyndsey, we have been best friends since we were teenagers, and I always had a crush on you. Things didn't work out as expected and we went our own ways. But we finally found our way back to each other because it was meant to be. We may only have been dating for a short time, but I know you better than I know anyone, and I love you."

Her eyes teared up, and she held her breath. This was

happening, and she was witnessing it firsthand instead of being told over the phone.

Kevin got down on one knee and all the women squealed and the men hooted and hollered..

"Since you're finally back in my life, I have never been happier. You're the Allie to my Noah, the Monica to my Chandler, the Beauty to my Beast, and the one person I can't imagine spending another day without my ring on your finger. Lyndsey Jeanette Jones, please don't make me wait another day to put this ring on your finger."

He opened the tiny case and placed a ring with a huge rock on her finger. Lyndsey blinked. "Kevin, this must have cost a fortune."

"You are worth every penny. Lyndsey, ill you put me out of my misery and be my wife?"

She nodded through her tears and jumped into his arms. They kissed as their friends clapped and he dipped her back to continue kissing her.

Brad whistled and clapped at the gesture, and they all wrapped them in a group hug. Once they backed away, Kevin raised Lyndsey's hand and showed off the ring.

Kevin cleared his throat to get everyone's attention. "Do you know what would really add to this moment right now?"

Lyndsey spread her fingers and gazed at her beautiful ring, then smiled at him. "I do not know if you can top this, but go ahead and try."

Kat was so happy to experience this moment with them. True love was still out there, and she would no longer settle for less. She loved being surrounded by all these couples so madly in love. Perhaps it was possible for her, too. She looked at Ethan and smiled to herself.

"Stop it, Kev, you are making me look bad," Brad said.

Kevin smiled, "A night swim like we did when we were teenagers."

Brad nodded. "I like that idea. You're on. Any other takers?"

Lyndsey stood up and peeled off her sweatshirt. "Let's do it. For old times' sake."

"It looks cold," Maddy said, clasping her hands together. "I don't even have my suit on."

"You don't need one," Brad said as he took off his shirt.

Lyndsey took a step toward Maddy and held out her hand. "Come on. West Sturgeon is the warmest of all the lakes. It's like bath water. Summer is coming to an end soon and we'll regret it if we don't."

"Fine. I'm in."

They all followed Lyndsey to the lake. The girls stripped down to their bras and underwear and the men to their boxers, then they ran into the water as fast as they could.

Kat was the last one in, behind Ethan. He walked slowly and turned to wait for her to catch up. The moonlight was bright enough to see the shadows of their friends as they dove under the water and started splashing each other.

Ethan pulled her closer. "Are you ready for this?"

"Yes."

She walked into the water, step for step with Ethan.

"It's so crazy, being back here with you. We were so in love and so wild. Not a care in the world."

Memories of the last time they went for a late-night swim made her smile. "Yeah, we were young and fearless."

"Before we jump in, I want to apologize to you for that kiss on the boat. I was a bit impulsive, but the truth is I never got over you. I knew it was now or never."

"Ethan, we have a history between us. I could have stopped you but I wanted the kiss as much as you did. It's not like it's going to happen again."

She wished it would happen again. He must be having second thoughts about her. Who was she kidding? They were teaming up to tell their daughter who they were. All the emotions surrounding them had made them impulsive and one thing led to another.

He was so good looking and that body was hard to keep her eyes off, but she could not go down that road again even if she had butterflies every time she talked to him. It was a normal reaction to her first crush.

"It's time," he said.

They counted to three and dove in. She heard screaming as she surfaced. Who was screaming? She looked to her right. Ethan was screaming. "Ethan, are you okay?!"

Twenty-Four

Ethan

He laid down in the sand and clenched his teeth as Kevin pulled out the piece of glass in his foot.

"Got it," he said, holding the glass by his fingertips.

"You wouldn't think there would be glass in the water. What's wrong with people throwing their bottles in the lake?"

"I've never heard of any glass over here," Maddy said. "I know we've found glass by Bimbo's, but never in our lake."

"I think it's getting better over there," Lyndsey said. "Not as bad as it used to be. People were throwing their bottles in the water to dispose of them before going into the restaurant."

They headed back to the fire. The glass in the sand ruined the moment and everyone got out of the water.

Ethan put on his shirt. "I had a great time, but I'm getting pretty tired. I should probably head back to Pine Beach." He took a couple steps with a limp.

"I'll give you a ride." Kat smiled. "I'm pretty tired myself and I'm not sure how far you will make it on that foot and with that limp."

"She'll give you a ride alright," Brad said with a grin, and everyone laughed.

She gave what she hoped was a casual laugh. "I'm the only person here not wasted. I don't mind."

She turned to Lyndsey and hugged her tight. "I am so happy for you." She winked at Kevin. "Both of you. It's about damn time."

Kevin wrapped his arm around Lyndsey and shook Ethan's hand. "Congrats you two. I can't say I'm surprised."

They headed to Kat's house to grab her car.

"Crap, I can't find my keys. Want to come in and help me find them?"

Ethan grinned. "You bet. This is what I'm good at."

She looked at him, confused. "Finding keys?"

He could find anything in a matter of seconds. He had a great memory and he was proud of it. "Finding things in general. It's my superpower."

She shook her head and turned away to search the living room. Ethan looked through drawers in the kitchen. No luck.

He came across a black book and opened it. It was Kat's mothers journal. He paged through it to make sure.

Kat came into the room and gasped.

She snatched it up from his hands. "My mom's journal. Why are you reading it? And where did you find it? I've been looking for it everywhere."

He held up his hands in surrender. "It was in the drawer. I was just wondering how it got here so fast since Andy just had it. When did he give it back to you?"

"What are you talking about? I lost it and I've been searching everywhere for it. I never gave it to Andy."

He shook his head in disbelief. "That night at Lyndsey's,

he told us he found out our daughter was in Side Lake from your mom's journal. He said you let him read it."

She cursed under her breath. "He took it. I knew it. I didn't want to believe it. How was I so stupid?" She opened it and flipped through the pages. "Pages are missing. Look here. They are ripped out at the end."

He leaned over her shoulder to look. "There definitely is. Was it not like this before?"

She shook her head and chewed on her thumb, deep in thought.

"But if he didn't give it back to you, how did it get in your house?"

She looked at him with a horrified expression. "He must have broken in. Maybe I left the door unlocked? I'm not sure."

She turned around and kicked something. Her keys flew across the room.

"Found my keys," she said, bending down to pick them up. "I must have dropped them."

"This is serious, Kat. How did he get in?"

"I don't know, but I'm not too worried about it. I'm sure he just wanted to drop it off and sneak away. All that matters now is I have it."

How could she not be nervous that Andy broke into the house?

"I don't want you staying here alone."

She stared at him with anger in her eyes. "Don't be so overprotective. You don't have to worry about me, Ethan. I'm not scared of Andy and I can take care of myself. He may be sneaky but he isn't dangerous."

He didn't want to argue with her, but he did worry about her. As they walked outside, lights flashed and blinded them.

"Ethan Iverson, who is this girl you're with? Are you in a relationship? Why were you arrested?"

"No comment!" He called out.

Kat looked over at him and then back to the cameras at the four men lined up in her backyard. "What's going on?"

"Why did you get arrested? Who did you beat up and why?"

"Just get in the car, I'll explain later."

Kat jumped into the driver's seat of her car and Ethan hurried to the passenger side.

She started the car. "Who the hell are those people and why are they asking about you getting arrested?"

"It's a long story. Let's lose them and then I'll tell you."

She nodded and screeched the tires as they drove off.

He watched her as she checked the rearview mirror. No lights. When she finally pulled into the resort, they were still silent, and nothing had been said between them since the minute they left her house.

"What was that?"

"I have been wanting to tell you but I haven't had the courage to do it yet. I wanted everything the way it was."

"Oh, really." She put her car into park and gave him a look that said she wanted answers, and she was not leaving until she got them.

"I haven't been exactly honest with you lately."

"Ok?"

"I'm not a struggling author."

"What?" She gasped. "You were lying to me? You aren't even a writer? What do you do then?"

That came out wrong. "No, I'm an author and a writer, but I'm a bit bigger than I may have led on."

She crossed her arms. "Then why have I never heard of you?"

He hated the way she was looking at him. Her blue eyes turned cold with a look of disdain. "I write under a pen name."

"What? No. You can't be serious. What's your pen name?"

"I write under Elizabeth Conrad."

Her mouth flew open, and she stared at him. "The Elizabeth Conrad? New York Times best-selling author, Elizabeth Conrad?"

He nodded in slow motion.

"I can't believe you didn't tell me. I have every one of her books your books. How could it be you? No way. Not possible."

He looked down. "I didn't tell anyone. I wanted it to be a secret. I wrote under a pen name for so many years. You see, females dominate the romance genre, and my agent convinced me years ago to use a woman's name because I'd have a better chance at success."

"I guess it worked. Gosh, Ethan. Any other secrets? I feel like you have a whole other life you never told me about."

Ethan's shoulders slumped. "I wanted to tell you. I did. I just—"

"But you didn't tell me." She studied him. "That was quite the way to find out."

"I screwed up. I'm sorry." He looked away.

"You realize this is going to be everywhere. We'll lose our chance to get to know our daughter now because not only will you be the talk of the internet, but the jail story will look so bad. Everyone will know. She will know."

He dug his fingers into his eyes.

"I don't know what to say to you," Kat murmured. "We need to tell her before she hears about you and your stupid arrest."

"Hey, that arrest was because of that crazy, jealous ex that you brought to Side Lake. I never laid a finger on him, and you know it."

Her face puckered.

He had gone too far. He tried to touch her shoulder, but she shrugged him off. "Just get out. Get out now."

Her anger made him frustrated. He did not mean for his secret pen name to come out that way. He was angry, and he needed her to understand. "Please, Kat, I need to explain."

"I need a minute to think. You lied to me and it better not get in the way of Emma."

He cleared his throat and tried again. "I'm sorry. Everything is going to be okay. We'll talk to Mark and Amy tomorrow, okay?"

"We have no choice now. You know, I was seriously considering staying here if she wanted to get to know me. Now I don't know if she'll want to get to know us if she thinks you're a criminal and a liar."

She put her car into drive, and he had no choice but to shut the door and let her go.

He screwed up again.

She was overreacting. Emma wouldn't think that. She knew him enough to know he was not a criminal. She would understand and he would fix this. He had to fix this or he would lose the two most important women in his life and that was not happening.

Twenty-Five

Kat

She sat down in front of the bookshelf and opened her mother's journal.

I was diagnosed with bipolar disorder today. My life is falling apart. I could end up in a psychiatric unit if I don't take my meds. I don't trust myself around my own daughter and I have been considering taking off and leaving her with my mom. I just can't love her the way I should. Every time I look at her, I see her father and it's killing me. She is this beautiful little girl, and I just can't do this anymore. I'm going to find her father and tell him the truth. He needs to know.

Wish me luck.
  XO Krystal

. . .

She turned the page.

After some investigating, I found out where he lived and worked in the Cities. I drove down and met him face to face at the restaurant where he was bartending while going to school. I got drunk and instead of telling him, we ended up sleeping together. We stayed up half the night talking about school and how he loved it there but he missed me. He asked how my daughter was and it tore me apart not to tell him she was his daughter, too. I knew I should, but I just couldn't. He'd probably drop out of school and move back here and then what? There was nothing for him here other than us. I didn't want him to throw away his future and everything he worked for. He didn't know the person I'd turned into. That my mental health was turning me into a psycho. Maybe someday I will have the guts to go back and tell him.

I'm so lost and such a chicken. I just don't know what to do anymore.

XO Krystal

The next entry was a year later. What happened to her mother that she never wrote an entry for a year? She had her suspicions.

. . .

I'm back. My mother died and I have to be the mother I struggle to be. I have to tell him. As soon as I have the strength, I'm going to tell him. It's his choice to make. Kat is so sad, and I don't know how to comfort her. I'm broken and numb. It's obvious she loved my mother more than she loves me. I'm not meant to be a mother and I don't know what to do.

Her next journal entry was fourteen years later...

How did I get here? She's pregnant and I can't do this anymore. I tried to help her get away from me so she wouldn't end up like me, sad and alone. It's too late to tell the love of my life he's a father and it's too late for me to be a good mother. I talked her into giving her baby up but it's to a great family that can't have kids of their own. They live in Side Lake so my grand baby will still grow up here. They don't know it was me that set this up and no one in Side Lake knows I have a grandchild. I just want Katrina to have the life I never had, and I finally got her away from me. My mental health continues to decline, and I just don't know who I am anymore. It was my job to make sure she didn't get pregnant like me, but I couldn't even do that right. Lord help me.

X Krystal

Tears streamed down her face, and her body trembled. She put the book down, unable to turn the page. Her emotions were on overload. She wanted to find her father and tell him the truth, but before she could do that she needed to find out if he knew now.

Aunt Bev would know the truth, and her mother was no longer around to stop her. She called her aunt.

"Kat, hey, what a great surprise. How are you? Is everything ok?"

"No, everything's not okay. I need to know about my father. I need to know how to find him."

Her aunt cleared her throat. "Katrina, your mom never wanted you to know who he was."

"Why? I'm an adult and she's gone. I want to know. Please tell me. Tell me where my father is. Please. She kept so much from me, took so much from me. I need this. Let me meet him and talk to him. Let me figure this out for myself. I need that closure."

Her aunt sighed. "I understand. I'll tell you who he is, and I think I know where he lives."

"Thank you."

"His name is Dennis Lind. He lives in Ely, near the boundary waters, I believe. At least he did a few years ago. I went with your mom because she wanted to see him."

"She saw him five years ago?"

Sarcastic laughter rung in her ears. "Your mom? No. She went there to see him from a distance. She couldn't talk to him. She said it hurt too much. Your mom was scared of everything."

"What did he look like? Is he married? Kids?"

"I'm not sure. We parked far away from his house. Your mom was looking at him through binoculars. She never told me much about him. You know your mom." She sounded disgusted. At least she was not the only one annoyed at her mother.

Her aunt and uncle were the closest people she ever had to parents, although she had a hard time getting along with her aunt when she was a teenager. She had trust issues. It took so long to rebuild all the walls her mother had torn down with her anger and judgement. When she graduated from high school, she finally accepted her aunt was someone she could trust and she opened up her heart to her more than she ever had.

"Thank you. Can you send me the address?"

"Yeah, I can do that."

"Thanks."

"Wait, don't hang up!" Her aunt shouted into the phone, catching her off guard.

"What is it? Is everything okay?"

"Yes, I just, um, wanted to make sure you're doing okay. I hate that I can't be there for you in Side Lake and you have to do this all on your own. It has to be so hard for you to be back there in that house."

"It's crazy but I'm okay. I've been healing a lot, and I've gotten to know my friends again. I forgot how great it is here. How everyone is family in Side Lake. Also, I found my mom's journal."

Her voice rose in disbelief. "Krystal had a journal? That's hard to believe."

"Yeah, I was pretty surprised myself. She was never the sentimental type."

"What does it say? Are you getting any answers?"

She paged through the journal as she talked. "She wrote about my father and that she never told him about me because she didn't want to stop him from going to college. Is that true?"

"Yeah, that's true. Your father was this popular, humble but handsome guy who loved your mother so much. Your mother loved him back just as much. After she got pregnant with you and didn't tell him, she became angry and hateful." She sighed. "Then she was diagnosed with bipolar disorder. She suffered some pretty bad manic episodes. It's no wonder she was so angry all the time. She struggled to take her meds and then flat out refused and self-mediated with alcohol which didn't help."

"Her journal is making more and more sense now. What else? Did she make you promise to never tell me the truth about my father and about her?"

"Worse," her aunt said. "She blackmailed me. She told me if I ever told you, she would take everything from me. Everything that mattered to me. You. And you know your mother, she wasn't a person who threatened and didn't follow through."

"Why do you think she tried so hard to cover up who my father is?" She paused. "Aunt Bev, is he a bad guy?"

"Not that I know of. I'm not really sure. All I know is that your mother had secrets and a lot of them. She didn't even tell me the whole truth."

The time had come to find her father and tell him the truth. Even if it did scare the crap out of her.

Twenty-Six

Ethan

He screwed up big time. Kat was angry and he worried what Emma would think of him. Sure, his books were popular, but how often were authors the highlight of social media? Only when there were secrets involved. He was arrested for the first time in his life and although he was innocent of the charges, it still did not look good. He looked guilty.

He went outside and wandered along the docks. No one was around this early in the morning. He wanted to call Kat and reach her voicemail so she would not hang up on him. He wanted her to listen to his explanation and the best shot he had was if he left her a voicemail.

He heard the beep and then her voice from behind. Kat was on the docks.

He turned around. "Kat, I was calling you to apologize for last night."

"I'm upset but the more I think about it, the more I realize this won't stop our daughter from wanting to be in our lives if she wants to be. It's a small town and everyone probably already knows you were arrested, and the charges were dropped. We have to work together if we're going to bring Emma into our lives and tell her the truth about us. We're her parents, Ethan, and it's time we stop wondering what she will say and just—'

A gasp from behind cut her off.

Ethan's heart fell. Had someone heard their conversation? They both turned around to see who it was.

His eyes met Emma's, and the air sucked out of his lungs and his eyes widened.

Emma bared her teeth, and her eyes protruded. "You guys are my parents? You hid this from me?" Her voice shook. "Ethan, I shared so much with you, why didn't you tell me? You both must think I'm such an idiot!"

He tried to speak, but the air caught in his lungs, and he started coughing. She stared at him, waiting for his reply.

Kat tried, but she looked frozen, too.

"Are you my father, Ethan?"

He nodded, then dropped his chin to his chest. "I didn't know how to tell you."

Kat stepped forward. "We were trying to figure out how to tell you, and we wanted to speak to your parents before we told you."

"Then how do you know for sure?"

"Your birthmark," he said pointing to Kat and then touching the back of his neck.

Kat turned around and lifted her hair. Emma gasped and covered her mouth. "If you're my parents, then why? Why did you leave me and why did you decide to find me after all these years?"

"We were teenagers in high school, too young to take care of you. And my mother ... well she arranged it all. Besides, we didn't know you were here. We didn't know you lived in Side Lake, or I would have come a long time ago."

Emma ignored her and turned to Ethan. "I thought you were my friend, Ethan. You knew you were my father this whole time and you never told me. I took you out kayaking, we had so much fun together. Why did you hide it from me?"

He took her by the shoulders before she could walk away.

She gave him an angry look, and he dropped his hold on her.

"I didn't know," he said. "Please let me explain before you walk away. Let us explain."

Her teeth clenched together. "I'm not like you. I don't just walk away. My parents taught me better."

Ouch. That was hurtful. It took him a minute to come back from that, but he understood. She was angry. She felt abandoned by them.

"Your mother and I—"

"My mother?" She cut him off. "What right does she have to be called my mother? Having sex doesn't make you a parent. Raising your daughter makes you a parent, and the two of you just walked away."

Her words hurt, and he knew Kat must be devastated. This was by far the worst pain he had ever felt. Did she really think this way? She hated them and resented them that much? His heart sank. "Listen, please."

She crossed her arms and tapped her foot. "I'm listening. What do you have to say, DAD?"

The word dad came out sarcastic, as if she did not consider him a father and she was right. He had not been there for her, nor did he raise her. Dad was a title earned, and he was just her biological father. What some people called a sperm doner. He was a dead-beat father. He never thought of himself that way until this moment.

"I know I deserve that, but please let me explain." He took a step forward and Emma took a step back.

Kat put her arm out to stop him from taking another step. "Ethan, stop. Let me talk."

"I don't want to hear any more excuses from either of you. Just go away. Let me be!"

Emma turned and stomped away.

"Wait, wait."

He jogged to Emma's side, Kat just steps behind.

She crossed her arms again. "I don't believe you suddenly figured out who I am. You were trying to get closer to me when we went kayaking, weren't you?"

He pinched his nose. "No. I didn't know then. I haven't known very long, I promise. I found out the day we were out in the water, when your friends were here and we were swimming. I knew something was familiar about you, but I had no idea you were my daughter. I swear. Not until I saw the birthmark on your neck."

"And I had a feeling the minute I met you." Kat's chin quivered. "I didn't have low blood sugar. I passed out from shock after realizing who you were. Please believe me."

The tears streamed down Emma's face. "Another lie?!"

He wanted to hug her, but that would only make her angrier.

"Please don't cry. I hate this. We wanted to talk to your parents first. We never should have waited this long." Kat wiped her eyes.

"But you didn't," Emma said. She turned her back to

them again. "I'm done talking to you guys." She climbed in her kayak and paddled away.

"Wait, don't go." He saw her life jacket on the ground. "At least take this with you. Please!"

She did not turn back, nor did she reply. She paddled away so fast she almost tipped the kayak over. He made his way to the dock and ran down it as fast as he could, Kat following his lead.

"Please, please just wait. Don't go," Kat said..

"Leave me alone," Emma said.

She was too far away for them to give her the life jacket. Ethan slid the other kayak into the water. Kat jumped in.

He grabbed two life jackets.

"She doesn't have a life jacket. Give her this one. I'll get on the paddle board and meet you out there. Go!" He gave her a push.

Kat sniffled. "What if she won't listen to me?"

"You got this, I know you do."

Kat was crying as she paddled so fast, she had to catch herself from going in a circle. She was not an expert kayaker.

She was wobbly and struggled to use the paddle without tipping the kayak. All he could do was watch as she struggled from a distance.

Twenty-Seven

Kat

The muscles in her arms burned, and she struggled to catch her breath. She kept yelling, "Emma! Emma!" As if she would just stop and wait.

She almost caught up but then Emma picked up her pace.

"Wait! Please! I need to explain. Please?" She gasped for breath, exhausted from all the paddling.

Two boats went speeding by way too close. She tried to paddle away before the wave swallowed her up, but the water came at her too fast to react. She tried to balance the kayak, but she was too weak and she lost control. The kayak flipped over.

She went under before she had time to take a breath. The water was dark, leaving her blind. She tried to make her way to the surface, but the waves kept coming and pushing her down. Her body took an involuntary breath, and she choked on the water. Her lungs collapsed. She needed air, needed to breathe.

A strange weakness overcame her. Was this what the end looked like? Her head finally surfaced, but she was too weak to take a breath. Her body sank into the dark water when she no longer had enough strength to fight.

Arms wrapped around her and pulled her to the surface.

She fought to stay awake and catch her breath, but she was so dizzy.

She coughed and her chest burned. Lips pressed against hers. She opened her eyes as someone rolled her on her side. She couldn't see, couldn't tell where she was, couldn't remember what happened.

Was she dead? Was this what it was like to die?

She was so close to getting to know her daughter. Now she never would. This was her punishment. Her punishment for selfishly abandoning her child.

She gasped for air, her lungs still not working. Someone turned her on her side.

A blue and yellow kayak came into view. Arms from the board reached for her.

"Mom, are you okay?" a shaky voice said.

The voice was as soft and beautiful as a princess. Her daughter's voice, she could feel it. Her eyes were open, but she only saw black spots. Her throat burned when she tried to speak.

She blinked and blinked, trying to focus, and then she saw him.

"Kat, It's me, Ethan. Are you okay?"

She rolled onto her back. He was kneeling on the paddle board. Her daughter was in the water, hanging onto the board. They were both with her. They were a family, even if just for a moment.

She sat up, almost falling off the board.

"Just stay still," Ethan said, slowly standing with a paddle now in his hand. They were headed for shore. Nowhere near Pine Beach.

"Where are we?"

"Under the bridge," Ethan said. "We're paddling to Riverside so we can call an ambulance. Just save your voice."

Good idea. Her voice was hoarse. She swallowed too much water. Her nostrils burned. She was too weak to get up. She touched her daughter's hand.

"Are you okay?" Emma said. She gazed into Kat's eyes. Her throat hurt too much to speak so she smiled instead.

"It's so weedy over here," Ethan said. "Emma, are you sure you're okay swimming in the weeds?"

The river veered off from the channel at Riverside and was weedy, shallow and mucky. Her daughter and Ethan had to be in weeds up to their necks, struggling to keep the paddle board from tipping.

"Weeds," she said, her voice more a croak.

"It's fine, mom, it's fine. I've been in worse. We have to get you to a doctor, now."

"Do you have your phone on you?" Ethan said to Emma.

"I did, but I'm pretty sure it's somewhere in the middle of Side Lake now."

Ethan let out a nervous laugh. "Same here."

"Are you okay, mom? Your skin is blue, especially your lips."

She heard the word mom. Sweet music to her ears. A word she never thought she would hear from her daughter. Her heart melted. She closed her eyes. Nothing mattered right now. The word mom circled in her head. She could die happy hearing those words from her sweet Emma.

. . .

"Mom? Mom, it's me. Can you hear me?"

Hearing those words was the best way she had ever been awakened. She blinked until her eyes opened. Every part of her body hurt, especially her lungs. She still struggled to speak, so she reached out and touched the side of her daughter's face. Emma pushed her face into Kat's hand. It was a miracle. Here they were together. She was touching her daughter for the first time.

Her eyes closed like there were weights on her eyelids. She struggled to open them again, but they were too heavy.

"Don't fight it, mom, just sleep."

She smiled again before closing her eyes.

She woke up to the sounds of Emma's voice.

"It's all my fault. I never should have taken off so fast."

"It wasn't your fault. That boat was in a no wake zone. It shouldn't have been going that fast."

Kat heard sobbing.

"I was just so angry. I thought running away would help. I'm sorry. 'm so sick of all the lies. I want to know the truth."

Kat opened her eyes. Emma was holding her hand.

Ethan leaned over her. "Hi. How are you feeling? You're in the hospital, everything is going to be okay."

She turned her head enough to lock eyes with Ethan. "Tell her."

He tilted his head. "Are you sure?"

"Yes. Tell her."

He turned to Emma and took a deep breath. "Where to start? Your mother and I were madly in love. Her mother was, well, a wicked woman with a lot of issues. She didn't want us together. She sent your mom away to her aunt's farm. Your mom left me a letter telling me she was pregnant. Her mother approached me with some paperwork and made me sign it. I was young and dumb, and I knew I couldn't care for you."

Emma wiped her eyes. "And when did you guys talk again?" She looked at Kat and then back at Ethan, making it perfectly clear who she was talking about.

Ethan glanced at her. "We didn't talk again until recently."

"All those years? Why not? What stopped you?"

Ethan smiled at her, then looked back at Emma. "I struggled to find her, I guess I didn't try hard enough."

"I'd say."

"I wrote her a letter and sent it to her mother's house, hoping she would get it, but she never did. I told myself if it was meant to be the letter would find her. I guess thinking that way made it easier."

"What easier?"

"Knowing I'd lost her."

Their daughter looked back and forth between them. Neither of them could look her in the eyes.

"You guys are still in love, aren't you?"

She raised her eyes, and Ethan raised his eyebrows. His face turned red.

Her defenses took over. "What? I didn't say that,"

"Look me in the eye and tell me you aren't in love with him," Emma said.

Silence.

So there was still something between them. It couldn't be love, but a connection of some sort. She would know if she loved him.

"It's been a lot of years and Kat and I haven't really talked about it. I would do anything for you, but I don't want this to be the way we discuss us. What matters the most to both of us is that we finally found you after all these years."

Emma sat down on Kat's bed. "I'm not going to lie, I was

so angry with you both and I still am. It hurts. I love my parents, but to know I had biological parents that gave me away always killed me. I grew up wondering who you were and why you did what you did."

"I get it," Kat whispered. "Don't believe for a second we gave you aways because we didn't love you. We were so young, still children. I knew I couldn't be the mother you needed. And neither of our parents were ready to help us raise a child. "

Emma turned her back on them and stared out the window.

"What you did today was amazing. You saved Kat's life," Ethan said. "You jumped right in, didn't think twice. And you scared the crap out of me. I realized I didn't know whether you could swim well enough to save someone, and then I started thinking about how much I've missed—we've missed. We hardly know anything about you and you're a piece of both of us."

That was one way to look at it. Emma was a piece of both of them. She wanted more than anything for their daughter to give them another chance. Her heart hurt at the thought of losing her again. She could not bear it.

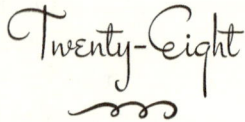

Ethan

He came so close to losing her. She could have drowned. Life was too short and in that moment, when he thought the worst, he realized he was madly in love with her. He had convinced himself he felt that way because they were so in love as teens, but it was much more than that.

As for his daughter, she was beautiful, kind, and sweet, like her mother. He wanted to be a part of her life, if she'd have him, but it would not be easy. She was worth the fight.

Emma turned around and faced them. "All my life, I wondered what you guys looked like. I made up this story in my head that you guys died and that's how I ended up with my parents. My parents are really great, but I never looked like them. We did family trees in school, and I made mine up. I always felt like I didn't fit in. But my parents were honest about my adoption, and they even celebrated my adoption each year." She wiped her eyes with the back of her hand.

Ethan took a step forward, not knowing if he should give her a pat on the back or a hug or what to do, so he just put his hands in his pockets. "I'm so sorry you felt that way. We wanted a better life for you than what we could give you. We were just so young."

She nodded but took a few seconds too long to say anything. "I know that, but it doesn't make it any less painful."

"That's understandable. I wish it could have been different," Kat said with a hoarse voice.

She deadpanned. "I need a little time to think about this, okay?"

Despite everything happening in her life, she smiled.

"I'm not saying you did anything wrong. I need to talk to my parents and sort it all out."

Beads of sweat ran down his forehead. "We understand."

"I'm so glad you're okay, Kat. I mean that," Emma said.

"Thank you for saving me," Kat said, reaching out for her hand.

Kat had tears in her eyes. She was hurting and thinking the same thing. Did Emma hate them? Would she ever forgive them or think of them as her parents? Would she ever talk to them again?

They both watched her walk out of the hospital room, and they stared at the door long after she left.

He grabbed the ice chips off the table next to her and handed them to Kat. She took them and put them into her mouth.

"I've been reading my mom's diary."

He waited for her to say more. Was it still a struggle to speak or were emotions overcoming her?

"She wrote about my father. I never knew my father."

He nodded.

"I finally know his name. It's Dennis." Her chin trembled." She kept it from me all this time. I thought if he never reached out, I never wanted to meet him." She coughed, trying to clear her throat, but it was getting hoarser as she spoke. "After seeing our daughter and knowing how hard it was for us , I've decided to find him and let him know my mother kept me from him. See if he wants to be a part of my life."

"Wow. Do you know where he lives?"

"My aunt thinks he lives in Ely, but I was hoping you could help."

"I can do that. I'll look into it for you. It may be as simple as googling him. Do you know his full name?"

She pushed a smile. "I do."

He grabbed her hand in his and sat down on the chair next to her bed.

"We'll get through this together. All of this. I'm not leaving your side."

She nodded and squeezed his hand.

Once Kat was at home in bed, under doctor's orders for plenty of water and rest, he got to work. He found out her father lived in Ely like her aunt thought. Ely was known for making Mukluks and where the Boundary Waters were located. It was so beautiful over there this time of year. He had not been there in so long.

He hung around while Kat slept close to eighteen hours straight. She woke up groggy, and a bit dehydrated. The first words out of her mouth were, "I need to find my father. I've waited my whole life to meet him."

"Rest and regain your strength, Kat."

"No, I won't waste another minute."

. . .

Ethan picked her up in his truck, and she was in a great mood. They were on their way to find her father. Her anxiety showed as she got into his car.

"Do I look okay?'

"You look beautiful."

She pulled at her black shorts. "Do you think I should wear pants?"

"No, it'll be eighty degrees in an hour. You're fine."

"Do you think I should wear tenner shoes in case we have to walk a lot?"

He shook his head, giving her a side glance as he drove. "Are you alright?"

She put her face in her hands, her happiness turned to nervousness. "No, I'm not okay. I'm not sure I want to meet him. Is that horrible?"

He thought about their daughter. This must have been the way she felt, except she never had a chance to anticipate meeting them for the first time. She overheard them talking about her. The thought made him queasy.

He put his hand on her leg, and she relaxed beneath his touch. "It's going to be okay. I'm right here. No matter what happens, you can say you tried."

She stiffened again. "But what if he doesn't want to meet me. What if he's not even there? What if we got the address wrong?"

"That sounds like a lot of what ifs that we can address when the time comes. If you decide not to meet him once we're there, that's okay. I won't make you. I'm just here for support. If he doesn't want to meet you, I'll punch him in the face, and if we got the address wrong, we'll spend the day shopping and maybe even take in the wolf museum. Nothing to worry about. Okay?"

She bit her nail and nodded as she stared out the window.

"I can't believe I'm doing this. Thank you." She placed her hand on top of his. His heart skipped a beat. Her hand felt so soft and warm.

They drove over a hill and a bright blue lake sparkled below them.

Kat gasped. "Oh, Ely is gorgeous."

Ely was a tourist town. People came from all over the world to see the boundary waters within close to a million acres of uncut forest. No motorized vehicles were allowed in the boundary waters, just canoes. People went camping without all the amenities of hotels or electricity. They slept in the peace and quiet of the great north woods in tents, with bonfires to stay warm.

"I camped here once a year, every year with my parents," he said. "They loved to unplug for a weekend and relax with family." He half-laughed. "Can you imagine kids doing that today? Anyway, I looked forward to weekends with my family. I had their full attention and my sister and I fought less when we were out here."

His GPS took them out to Echo Trail and as they turned into a long, winding driveway, Kat started biting her nails again.

He put his hand on her thigh, and she exhaled.

"It's now or never, I guess."

He pulled up to a log house and put his truck into park. He turned his head to look at her. She made no attempt to get out. He turned off the car, opened his door, and made his way around the truck to open her door for her.

He held out his hand to help her down. "You ready?"

She stared at him, like a deer in headlights. "Will you come with me?"

His eyes softened. "Do you want me to?"

She nodded, and he helped her out and shut the door.

"Well then, I guess I'm coming with you."

A black Ford F150 sat in the driveway. The house was small but gorgeous, with a white picket fence. Quiet woods surrounded the house.

As they walked up the three steps to the front door, Ethan grabbed her hand and squeezed it. She squeezed back and cast a nervous glance in his direction. She dropped his hand and rang the doorbell.

After a few seconds, she turned to him. "I don't think he's home. Let's go."

Just as she turned around, the door opened and a young girl around the age of six gave them a toothy smile.

"Hi there. Is Dennis home?"

"That's my granddaddy," she said in a high-pitched voice.

Kat's face turned white.

The little girl disappeared, and a man came to the door. He was about six feet tall, and his hair was salt and pepper colored. He was handsome with a small dimple in his chin like Kat, and obviously in great shape.

"Can I help you?"

"I'm, I'm—"

He studied her face. "I'm sorry, it's just that you look an awful lot like someone I used to know."

With a shaky voice, she said, "That person doesn't happen to be a woman by the name of Krystal, does it?"

He stared at her, his mouth open. He backed up unsteadily, tripping over the rug, and caught himself on the wall behind him.

"Are you okay?" a woman said from deeper in the house. "Who' at the door?"

He looked over at the woman and then back at Kat, pointing.

Kat and Ethan exchanged worried glances.

A woman poked her head around the door. She crossed her arms and glared at Kat. "Who are you, and what are you doing here?"

Kat tried to peek behind the woman to make sure her father was alright. Ethan tried too, but the woman completely blocked his view.

"I'm Kat and this is Ethan."

They both held out their hands to shake her hand, but the woman put her hand behind her back.

"What do you want?"

"I'm Dennis's daughter."

The woman stared at her, her expression unreadable. Ethan held Kat's hand for support. What would this woman do?

Was this blonde woman Dennis's daughter or wife? It wasn't clear. Whoever she was, she had an emotional attachment to Dennis.

The woman shut the door and took a step toward Kat. Kat stepped back in response. The woman backed Kat into the railing and put her finger in her face.

Ethan took a defensive step toward Kat, but Kat waved him off.

"My father is the most honest and caring man, and if he had another daughter, I would know about it. I'm not sure who you are or what you want, but I'm not buying it."

"Please, let me explain."

He did not like how close the woman was to Kat's face. She should back off, but Kat was letting her bully her.

"You think you're the first person who has tried to scam my father?" She laughed. "He's been through enough, and he doesn't need this. Get the hell off his property and don't you ever come back, you hear me?" She turned around to walk inside.

"But—"

She glared at Kat. "Get out or I'm calling the police."

Kat burst into tears when they got into the truck. The woman he assumed to be Kat's sister watched them until they drove away.

He put his arm around her shoulder as much as he could while driving, and she cried even harder. He pulled over and reached for her. "Here's a tissue."

She took it in her hand and wiped her nose and eyes.

"How are you doing?"

It took her a minute to calm down enough to speak. "She wouldn't even give me a chance to explain. I mean, that had to be my sister, Ethan. I have a sister and she's awful."

"I don't think she's awful. I think she's protective. They're in shock. Give them some time."

She nodded as tears spilled from her eyes. "But how will they come around when they don't even know who I am or where I live?"

"Trust me, they'll find a way."

Twenty-Nine

Kat

Kat to hoped Emma was working the supper crowd at Bimbo's when she headed to Pine Beach. She did not want her to be there when she and Ethan finally spoke to Amy and Mark.

She still felt pretty numb after the altercation with her stepsister, but she pushed the sordid affair out of her mind. It hurt too much and she had other problems she needed to be focusing on right now.

She sent a text to Ethan, letting him know she had arrived and pulled her car up to cabin five. Ethan was on the deck doing pushups and had not seen her message. From the sweat stains on his gray shirt, he must have just finished a run.

She shut her car door, startling him enough to make him jump to his feet. He wiped his wet forehead with a towel and made his way over to her. "Why must you always scare the crap out of me when I am doing pushups and listening to my music?" he said as he put his arm around her.

She shivered beneath his touch.

"How are you doing?"

"I should ask you the same question. Looks like you were letting off some steam." She muffled her giggle with her hand.

He looked down at his damp shirt.

"Yeah, let me grab a shirt. Wouldn't want you to run off again."

A flush spread across her cheeks. "I was running away from the horrible body odor protruding out of your pores that day." She stepped forward to smell him. "You don't smell incredibly terrible today. Let's get this over with now."

He stared so deep into her eyes, her skin felt like a wildfire burned her from head to toe. She shook it off and followed him inside.

The cabin smelled of cedarwood and thyme, and was cool after the hot, muggy air outside.

"Are you ready for this?"

She shuddered. "As ready as I'll ever be. You think they know already?"

She stared at his back, the muscles bulging as he reached for a shirt in the closet. She wanted more than anything to kiss his shoulders and run her hands over every muscle on his back. She shook away the thought, she was doing it again. This was not why she was here. She was here for their daughter. She blamed her sexual thoughts on her nerves. He was a pleasant distraction from what they were about to face.

She closed her eyes and took a calming breath before answering. "I don't know. I'm not sure if I hope they already know or not."

"Very true. I don't want to break it to them, but then

again if they already know, they may be pissed at us for not telling them."

Ethan grabbed her hand and squeezed it. They held hands until they reached Amy and Mark's front door.

He held his hand in front of the door, ready to knock. "Ready?"

He waited for her to give him the go ahead, which she did with a smile and a nod.

She held her breath as Emma's mother answered the door. "We've been waiting for you. Come in."

Amy's eyes appeared cloudy and her face stern.

Kat grabbed onto Ethan's hand for support. She was so glad she was not doing this alone.

Her heart pressed against her lungs, and she struggled to catch her breath.

"Take a seat."

Their house was tidy but small. Lyndsey told her they were minimalists and they liked to keep a beautiful, tidy home full of creative grace.

Amy picked up a pitcher of lemonade and poured them both a glass without asking if they wanted one. She really was waiting for them.

"I know who you are," Amy said. "But I haven't seen either one of you since you were teenagers."

Her husband, Mark, walked into the room and sat on the couch beside his wife. "We knew you both really well back then."

Not even a hint of a smile crossed his lips. He had big bags under his eyes. They both looked drained, exhausted.

"Emma was a mess after she found out about the both of you. We knew it was a possibility you would come back some day," Amy said, tapping her nails on her glass.

"And we told her she was adopted as soon as she was old enough to understand," Mark said, his voice unsteady.

Amy flashed him a sad smile, and their hands joined.

"We never wanted to keep you a secret from her, but your mother insisted. She thought you were too young to be a mother, and she wanted to protect you from the pain." Amy wiped away tears with the back of her hand.

Kat gasped. "You knew we were her parents?"

"Not exactly. Your mother set up a closed adoption but stated she wanted someone in the area. The adoption agency found us, and I ran into your mother one day. She knew who Emma was the minute she saw her. That's when she told me the truth about it all."

"So she met Emma?" Kat said.

"Yes, the first time was when Emma was little. She was pretty shook up."

Kat held her chest and took it all in.

"When we heard your mother passed away, we knew you'd be back in town, but we weren't sure you would recognize Emma or know she was around here. Your mother said she didn't tell you anything to avoid causing you more pain. We weren't sure if the two of you wanted to know or not." She sighed. "We debated telling you."

"She's the spitting image of Kat," Ethan said. "It was easy to see. That birthmark."

"Yeah, that's what your mother said. I just wish you guys talked to us first so we could have been there. It was a lot for her," Amy said, her eyebrows drawn together.

"We wanted to talk to you before we said anything to Emma, but she overheard us at the dock," Kat said.

Amy nodded. "I know. Emma told us what happened. She was in shock. It's been hard for her, but we want you to know we support any relationship she wants to have with you and we're glad she met you."

Mark stared into his hands as he fidgeted with his fingers. "This isn't easy for us. She's our daughter, but we want her to be happy. She's struggled so much with wanting to know who her biological parents were and why you gave her up. I just hope she finds whatever it is she needs from meeting you."

Kat's stomach twisted in knots. "We appreciate that. Thank you."

"We want her to find some peace in all of this. If she's happy, we're happy," Mark said.

This meeting and the whole affair was obviously hard for them. Their words seemed almost scripted.

Amy crossed and uncrossed her legs. "Promise you won't disappear out of her life if she decides she wants to build a relationship with you."

"We're here to stay," Ethan said, and Kat nodded.

Kat could only imagine how hard this must be for them. They raised her daughter as their own. They were there when she was sick, and they were there for school conferences, and they knew everything about her. She and Ethan knew nothing. They were never there. They gave up their rights to be a part of her life and it haunted her every day since she gave her up.

Would she have been a good mother if she kept Emma at such a young age? Probably not. Not like them. What they were doing was selfless. It had to hurt that Emma's biological parents popped into her life after all these years to claim the title of mom and dad. Were they really her mom and dad? Emma's adoptive parents seemed like good people with big hearts. She was so grateful they were there to raise her daughter when it was impossible for her to do so.

"I want to say thank you. It's obvious how much Emma means to you, and we're here because we love her. We were young and not ready to be parents. It seems like she has had a good life with loving parents who have been here for her through all the good and bad times. We really can't express our gratitude enough. Thank you."

Her words made them both cry.

"Oh, Kat. I remember you as a child and up until you moved away. You were always so sweet and your mother was so hard on you." Amy removed her hand from her husband's grip and reached for Kat's hand. "You've obviously grown up to be a wonderful person."

She looked right into Kat's eyes with kindness.

"I'm sorry for everything you must have gone through. You were so young. It couldn't have been an easy decision. Your mother said she didn't know if she did the right thing, but you were too young and it would have ruined your life to raise a child."

"Just to clarify, it wouldn't have ruined my life, but I knew I wasn't ready to raise a child. Thank you for raising her as your own. It's obvious you did a wonderful job with her."

Amy pursed her lips together, then opened them, her eyes beaming with pride. "Thank you. That means more than you know."

Her heart fluttered.

Mark leaned forward to grab a tissue and handed it to his wife. "Thank you. It means a lot. Really..." He patted his wife's back as she wiped her eyes.

"We're sad because this is hard for us, but we're glad you're here. It's what's best for Emma. Just please don't leave us in the dark. She's old enough to make her own decisions. We just need you to promise you won't break her heart."

"Never," they both said.

"I've thought about her every day since the day she was born. I didn't have much choice in the matter, but it broke me having to give her up. I'm grateful for the chance to get to know her now," Kat said. "Whatever that may look like for her. We aren't here to take her away from you. That was never what we were trying to do."

Amy stood up and hugged her. "Thank you. That makes us feel better. She's stubborn but she'll come around. Don't give up on her."

She could no longer hold back the tears as they streamed down her face. She hugged the woman who was there for her daughter when she could not be. "Thank you for letting us into your home and trusting us."

"Thank you for coming to see us," Amy said softly.

Out in the tall garden in front of their house, she leaned over, her hands on her knees, and began panting. She tried to catch her breath but it was impossible.

Ethan patted her back. "Deep breaths, deep breaths."

She tried but it got worse.

"I—think—I'm—dying."

He grabbed her hand and put it on his chest. "Focus on my heartbeat."

Touching him just made her heart beat faster.

She was choking on air. Who chokes on air? She was dying, but she could not die, not without resolving the issues with sweet Emma. Not when she finally found her.

Ethan picked her up and put her on his shoulder. He ran to his cabin and set her down on the couch.

"Here, breathe into this." He held out a brown lunch bag.

Black spots flashed across her eyes and she was still panting. The bag inflated then deflated. Inflated then deflated. Her breathing finally slowed. Ethan was rubbing her back and holding her hair up to cool her neck.

"Are you feeling better?"

She coughed. "What the hell was that? That's never happened to me before."

"It looked like a panic attack. You have a lot going on right now. Are you okay?"

She shook her head and her eyes rolled back. "I'm exhausted."

"Why don't you lay down on my bed?"

His bed? That would not help her breathing stabilize.

"No—I—"

He picked her up and carried her into his room and lay her on top of his bed. "This is non-negotiable. You need to rest."

She did not have the energy to argue, and his bed was so comfortable. He lay down on the bed beside her and rubbed her back.

She wanted to protest and give him every reason why he needed to stop, but she was too exhausted to fight him. Especially when she felt so happy in his arms and in his bed.

Thirty

Ethan

Kat slept the rest of the day and woke up at four in the morning when he was just falling asleep. He enjoyed every moment with her in his arms. The way she moaned in her sleep and made a quiet clicking noise. His heart ached for her, but he was a perfect gentleman.

He was too scared to move and wake her when his arm fell asleep. It no longer had any feeling, and he was unable to use it without physically moving it with his other hand.

Kat opened her eyes and jumped out of bed. "What happened? Where am I?"

He grabbed his numb arm and stood up. "You passed out. Everything is okay."

She pulled at her clothes as if making sure she was dressed. "Everyone will think we had a rendezvous or something if they find out I was here all night."

"Take a breath, Kat. I don't want you to have another panic attack."

That only seemed to make her panic more.

"I had a panic attack?" she said, rubbing the back of her neck. "That's never happened to me before."

Her breathing picked up speed. "Here, sit down," he said, patting the bed. "You need to relax. I don't care about what anyone else thinks. I'm worried about you."

She stopped and stared at him.

His eyes narrowed. "Did I say something? I'm sorry if I offended you."

She rubbed her eyes and then ran them down her face with both hands, as if she wanted him to disappear.

"No. It's not that. I—" She groaned. "There has been so much this week with Emma and my dad and everything with my mom. It's catching up to me."

Tears were next, so he wrapped his arms around her. She sniffled into his shoulder, and he held her tight.

"It's going to be okay. Let me help, okay? I hate seeing you like this."

She backed her head away, but stayed close to him. He expected her to turn away, but instead, she wiped her eyes and smiled at him. Then she laughed, hard. Should he laugh with her or pull her back in for a hug? Mascara ran down her cheeks. He wiped the streaks away with his thumb.

She stopped laughing, and her body stiffened. They leaned closer until their lips met. The first kiss was soft and slow until it picked up and they were both raging with need.

He had been waiting for her his whole life, but he refused to let his hormones and her vulnerable state make her regret moving so fast.

It took everything he had to stop the kiss.

She looked confused, upset. Then offended, as she backed away.

"I'm sorry. I guess I was reading this wrong. I should go."

He grabbed her hands. "No. Stay. Please stay."

A flash of embarrassment crossed her face, and she looked down.

He reached for her chin and lifted it. "Look at me."

She did, right into his eyes.

A part of him was breaking, having to stop what he wanted so badly. "I'm not stopping because I want to. I'm stopping this because I have to."

She sighed. "I feel so stupid. I can't believe I ever thought this would work between us. We were children when we dated. We have nothing in common anymore."

This time she did turn away, but he grabbed her hand and turned her back toward him and pulled her close. "Don't you do this. I would take you and throw you on that bed right there and make love to you if I thought you wouldn't regret it the minute we were done."

"Sounds like I'm not really missing out on much if I'd regret it the minute we were done."

He shook his head and grinned. "You and that mouth."

He pushed her down on his bed and straddled her, holding her hands behind her head. "Trust me, it will happen, and it will be the most unforgettable sex you've ever had."

She lifted her head, just inches from his lips. He shivered.

She whispered, "Sounds like a lot of promises for a man who is running away."

She flipped him over, now on top of him.

"I'm glad to see you've overcome your anxiety."

"Listen here, Mr. Iverson. I'm anxious because I've lost the mother who hated me and made my life a living hell. A sister I never knew I had and a father I dreamed my whole life of finding have rejected me. I found my daughter who wants nothing to do with me because I abandoned her the day she was born, and I just had my very first panic attack because I came back to the place I despise the most and promised myself I would never return to." She paused, as if contemplating whether to continue.

"Once I returned here, I was reunited with the one and only man I ever loved, but whom I haven't seen since I was a teenager and you think I'm making an impulsive decision by kissing you? You think I'd regret that in the morning?" She sat up and jumped off him. "I want to make love to you and see if the spark is still there because the possibility that we may still be soul mates is something I can't stop thinking about. I know that sounds stupid but—"

He pulled her down onto the bed with him. They rolled together back and forth, kissing. He could feel the electricity in every part of his body, just like when they made love for the first time all those years ago.

He promised himself right then and there he would never lose her again and if she was ready, then he would not deprive her any longer.

He pulled open her blouse, the buttons popped off and flew across the room. One hit him between the eyes, but he shook it off. She bit his lip and took off his shirt.

He slowly undressed her. Her body was every bit as perfect as it was when they were teenagers, but age made it even more perfect. He kissed her neck all the way down to her c-section scar and then stopped, pulled away, and kissed it even more tenderly. She was so beautiful.

He kissed his way up to her lips and stared into her eyes before it was her turn to undress him. She took her time, staring into his eyes that were begging her for more.

They made love until they passed out, and then he slept with the love of his life snuggled up against him.

When he woke up in the morning, he reached out for her, but all he found was the empty spot next to him on the bed. He searched the house, but she was not in the bathroom or in the kitchen.

He headed back into the bedroom to put on his boxers so no one would see him through the thin shades and huge windows.

He peeked out the door, but she was nowhere to be seen. He went back to the bedroom and collapsed on the bed. Did she regret last night? Did this happen too fast? Should he have waited to make love to her? His heart sank. He could not lose her again. He would not allow that to happen.

He grabbed her pillow to cover his face, and something dropped on his face. He grabbed the piece of paper and read it.

Ethan,

I can't do this right now. Last night was amazing, but I can't handle whatever this is. I'm hurting so badly, and I'm not ready to get into another relationship. We need to work together for Emma, but this thing with us is over. Please don't try to talk to me. I need some time. Thank you for being such a good friend, but that is all we will ever be.

. . .

Kat

She spent her whole life running, and she was doing it again. It hurt, but her reluctance would not stop him. He knew what he needed to do. He picked up his phone and spent the next thirty minutes searching for what he needed online.

"Bingo." He punched in the number and called.

"Rachel? Don't hang up. I need to explain something to you, and if you hang up the phone, I'll keep calling you, so save yourself some time and listen to what I have to say."

Kat

By the time she walked all the way to Turtle Creek Road, her shirt was soaked with sweat and her toes had blisters from her shoes. She stared down the road, not feeling like going back to her mother's house. She kept walking until she reached Lyndsey's doorstep.

She knocked.

Lyndsey opened the door and gave her a concerned look. "Kat, are you okay?"

She shook her head and broke down.

"Oh, sweetie, what happened?"

Lyndsey wrapped her arms around her friend, and Kat sobbed until she ran out of tears.

"Let's go inside and you can tell me what's going on. Okay?"

She sniffed and nodded.

She sat at the end of Lyndsey's couch under a warm blanket and told Lyndsey about her father and her sister.

Lyndsey put the box of Kleenex in front of her. "So, where did you walk here from? You're soaking wet."

Now or never. "Pine Beach," she said, biting her lip.

Lyndsey jumped to her feet. "You've got that a guilty tone in your voice, Katrina," she said, pointing a finger at her. "And a guilty look on your face, too! Tell me you slept with Ethan. Please tell me you did."

She nodded.

"Katrina, you naughty girl. I didn't know you had it in you. The old Kat is back. Tell me everything." She sat down on the couch, glowing with joy.

"It was everything I remembered, but so much better."

Lyndsey squealed and covered her mouth with her hands.

Kevin walked into the living room, buttoning his uniform.

Kat smiled. "Hello, Kevin."

"What are the two of you so giddy about in here?"

Lyndsey raised her eyebrows at Kat as if asking her if she could tell him.

She rolled her eyes and nodded.

"Kat and Ethan hooked up last night."

"It's about damn time. Does this mean you're staying in Side Lake? Because if you don't, my fiancé here is going to have a breakdown."

Lyndsey threw a pillow at him. "Kevin!"

"What? It's true."

He picked up the pillow and playfully hit Lyndsey with it. Lyndsey laughed and fell off the couch. He straddled her between his legs and started tickling her.

"Stop it, Kev! I have to pee."

"Get a room, you two," Kat said. She threw another pillow at them.

Kevin got off Lyndsey and threw the pillow at Kat. He returned his attention to Lyndsey and grinned. "Don't want you to have an accident, so I'll listen to you this time."

He started walking away, and Lyndsey jumped on his back. He gently lowered her to the floor, tickling her again. She squealed and tried to squirm away, but he held her steady.

He poked her twice in the stomach. "You done?"

She laughed but was out of breath. "My stomach hurts. Truce, truce, Kevin!"

He stood up to tuck in his shirt, but he kept looking back to make sure she was not surprising him again.

"Kat, keep this wild woman under control while I'm gone, okay?"

Kat laughed. "You guys are so cute."

He put his duty belt on and kissed Lyndsey goodbye.

Lyndsey wiped smeared makeup from her eyes and sat down on the couch.

She looked at Kat. "Are you two official now then?"

"Not exactly. I left before he woke up."

"No, Kat! Why?"

"I was scared. There is so much I need to tell you."

Lyndsey leaned forward on the couch. "But you can't just leave without talking to him."

Kat put her head down. "I'm not that horrible. I left him a note."

Her expression turned to concern. "Please don't tell me you left him another Dear John letter."

She forced a smile that came off flat. "Okay, I won't tell you."

"Seriously?" she said through clenched teeth. "Why?"

"I don't know. I was scared, and like I said, there is so much you don't know."

She crossed her arms. "This better be good. You can't keep doing this to him."

"Ethan and I figured out who our daughter is."

Lyndsey gasped. "You're kidding me. How? When?"

She took a deep breath and held it until she was ready to speak, then let out a loud exhale. "Well..."

She told the entire story about Emma and her parents. Then she told Lyndsey about meeting her father and her sister.

When she was done, Lyndsey wrapped her fingers in her hair, deep in thought. "That's a lot, Kat. Wow. I need a minute just to digest this."

"How do you think I feel?"

Lyndsey paced back and forth in front of the couch. "This is so unbelievable. First of all, I know Emma really well. She's a great girl, and it sounds like Mark and Amy are on board for you to be a part of her life, which doesn't surprise me. They've always been honest about Emma being adopted, and they're open minded. It's no wonder their resort does so well."

"I can see that."

"Is their son Dave adopted too?"

Lyndsey shook her head. "They thought they couldn't have kids, so they adopted Emma and immediately got pregnant with Dave. It was a miracle, really."

"I'd say."

"Kat, if you want to fight for Emma, I think I can help. As for Ethan, don't let him slip away again. I know you're scared, but he's Ethan. The two of you belong together. From your bickering to the sweet looks the two of you give each other when you think no one is looking, we all knew it was a matter of time before the two of you got back together. Don't let him slip away, Kat. Don't push everyone away like your mother did."

Kat's phone rang. She looked at the number, 612 area code. She silenced it, the number unfamiliar.

Lyndsey put her hand on Kat's shoulder. "I can't help you with Ethan, Kat. Only you can make that choice. But I can help you with Emma."

Kat shook her head. "Emma is something I need to fix on my own. She's my daughter, Lyndsey. I need to fix this."

Lyndsey smiled. "I can't believe she's your daughter. Now that I know, I see she's the spitting image of you. How did I not know?"

"You only see what you want to see, I guess. Why would you put it together when you never had a reason to suspect it? I hope you don't hate me for keeping all this from you."

Lyndsey grabbed her hand. "Kat, you and I have kept in contact, but it hasn't been the same since you left. I don't expect you to tell me everything that happens in your life unless you want to. Our friendship isn't about sharing everything, it's about knowing the other person will be there when you need them, and that's what I'm doing."

"Thank you, Lyndsey. I've never had a friend like you before. I've never had friends like the ones I have here at the lake. As for me living here, I don't think I can ever leave now. This is where I belong." After the words came out of her mouth, she knew they were true.

They hugged, and as they pulled away, Lyndsey grabbed both of her hands again. "Since you're here, there's something I've been meaning to ask you."

"What?"

"Will you be my maid of honor?"

Speechless, she jumped up and down and hugged Lyndsey. "Yes! Yes! I'm honored."

"I still can't believe I'm marrying Kevin Finney. It's crazy, right?"

"It's not crazy at all. The two of you were meant to be. I hope I can take that leap one day and let someone in like you have."

"Maybe that someone is right in front of you. You need to take a leap of faith and trust that he will catch you when you fall."

She had a good point, but it was easier to say than to listen. She was scared Ethan would not stay around, that he would leave her like everyone else in her life. Avoiding him and protecting her heart was easier.

"And Kat, I'm not offended that you didn't tell us Ethan was a famous author, and the paparazzi were at your door. The two of you looked pretty good. And a movie deal? Can you imagine?"

"Does everyone know?"

"Of course everyone knows," Lyndsey said.

"Are they angry?"

"God no, the town is so excited about the publicity, and everyone wants to be an extra in the upcoming movie."

That brought a smile to Kat's face. "Ethan doesn't know if the movie is for sure yet."

"Oh, it sounds like a done deal, according to the internet anyway."

Ethan

Ethan hung up the phone with his agent and went for a long run-down highway five, all the way to Greenrock Road and back. He left his earbuds and phone behind so he had no distractions, and he could run and think.

He agreed to an interview, and the paparazzi disappeared. A couple of photos and an article were all they were looking for. He was free to run and be alone without having to answer any more questions.

This time, he did not turn onto Turtle Creek Road. His heart was broken. She was gone again, and he could not keep chasing her. He had already told her how he felt. Now she needed to decide whether he was worth being with. She wanted them to make love last night even though he resisted. She convinced him. And that letter—that was the second time she left him with a letter instead of facing him.

He slowed to a walk and went through Pine Beach all the

way to his cabin. Someone was sitting on his steps. Was Kat back to apologize? He highly doubted it. Maybe she was there because she wanted to come up with a plan to get Emma back. That was the only reasonable explanation.

The woman stood up. It was Emma.

He jogged the rest of the way to her. "Hey," he said.

"Hey, Ethan—dad. I'm not sure what to call you, to be honest."

"Whatever feels right," he said, toweling off his face and neck. "Sorry, I just went for a run and I'm drenched."

She laughed. "I can see that. I'm here because I wanted to tell you I'm sorry. I've been thinking a lot, and I believe you didn't know who I was. I was just caught off guard. The more I thought about it, the more I realized that nothing you or Kat said could have calmed me down. I want you both to be a part of my life and I know it isn't easy."

"We would be honored. No pressure, but we want to be a part of your life. You get to choose how much."

She stared at the ground and dug her toe into the gravel. "I'm not sure what I want, but I'd like to start off spending some time with you both and getting to know you better."

"I'd love that. I know Kat would, too."

She stuffed her hands in her back pockets.

"Do you want to come inside and chat? I could call Kat. I'm sure she'd love to see you. I think she's at home. We could call her or go over there."

She smiled. "Yeah, let's go over there. Would it be weird if we just showed up?"

"No, not at all. She'll be so happy to see you. Trust me."

His stomach clenched at the thought of seeing Kat after the night before, but bringing Emma over might break the awkwardness between them. After they met with Emma, they no longer needed to be a team. They could see Emma on their own. Kat would be happy with that, but it hurt knowing they would never be together. Kat would never trust him.

Kat was carrying a box to the open garage when they pulled up. She saw him at first and shook her head until she saw Emma. She walked over to them as they got out of the car.

"Emma?"

"Hey, Kat," Emma said shyly.

"I was packing up the rest of my mom's stuff. Do you want to come inside and have a cup of tea?"

Emma looked at Ethan and then back to Kat. "I'd love that."

"I'll, um, let the two of you have some time together." Ethan said. "Some girl time."

Kat did not want him there. He saw it on her face.

Emma gave him a sad look and Kat blinked and said, "Ethan, you should come in. It would be great for the three of us to talk. You don't have to go."

She really wanted him to stay. That was hard to believe.

Emma smiled. "Dad, stay."

Dad? "I'm not going anywhere." He followed them inside, a smile on his face.

"So, are you still planning on moving back to the Cities and selling grandma's house?"

He loved that she felt comfortable enough to call him dad and Kat's mother her grandmother. It showed she accepting them as her family. Amy was right. Emma had enough love in her heart for everyone.

"I guess I'm not sure," Kat said. "My mom and I weren't

close, so to be honest I didn't plan on living here, but now that I found you and my friends again, I don't think I'll be able to leave. I never let myself believe I was happy here."

Emma smiled genuinely. "Your mom was an alcoholic, right?"

"She was. She drank a lot because she was struggling with her mental health."

"I still wish I could have gotten to know her," Emma said. "She was my grandma."

"Hang on a second," Kat said. She headed into the other room. When she came back, she handed the journal to Emma.

"What's this?"

"It's my mother's journal. I found it when I was cleaning. There are a few pages torn out at the end, but I already read it. Maybe this will help you to better understand her."

She paged through the book and looked back at Kat. "Did it help you understand her?"

"It really did."

The doorbell rang, and Kat got up to answer the door. "It's probably Lyndsey. I'll be right back."

"This is a really nice house," Emma said. "I can't believe she'd want to sell it."

"I think she has a lot of sad memories here," Ethan said. Kat was gone for several minutes. He became a little concerned. "Hold on, I'll check on Kat and make sure everything is okay. I'll be right back." He walked to the front door. Kat's father, her sister, and a little girl stood in the entrance. The sight stopped him in his tracks.

Kat had the biggest smile on her face. "Ethan, would you get Emma? My dad wants to meet her."

He smiled, and when he turned around, Emma was already standing behind him.

Kat put her hand on Emma's lower back. "Rachel, dad, Rosie, meet our daughter, Emma. Emma, this is your family."

He fought not to lose it. All Kat ever wanted was family, and now her front entryway was filled with her family.

Emma surprised them by hugging them all.

"Please, come in, everyone," Kat said, moving out of the way so they could walk past her.

"Thank you so much for inviting us, Ethan," Rachel said.

Kat made eye contact with him and mouthed thank you.

He nodded back at her.

"Your boyfriend here told us the truth, and I want to apologize. Your mother always said you weren't mine, and I never second guessed her," Dennis said.

"And he never told me because he didn't know," Rachel said. "I know it may not seem that way, but I'm so excited to meet you, Kat. I've always been an only child. I hope you can forgive me for the way I acted. Once my dad explained that it was a possibility and Ethan called us and explained everything, I knew you weren't lying."

"I'm so glad you came," Ethan said to them both. "We're all dying to hear more about you. Tell us about yourself, Dennis."

He cleared his throat. "I was a lawyer for many years and last year I retired so I could do some traveling and spend time with my family, but I still take a few cases here and there."

"Don't let daddy fool you, he's the best lawyer around, and I don't think he will ever fully retire."

He laughed. "That's probably true. I do love what I do. The reason Rachel was so quick to anger when you showed up was because I had a partner involved in some shady stuff who tried to pull me down with him. He has tried to scam me since."

"He was very jealous and dad pulled out of doing business

with the guy before he could drag him under. It was shady stuff," Rachel said.

"I thought you were a little young to be retired," Ethan said. "Are you married?"

He shook his head and tapped his fingers on the table. "No. Rachel's mom and I divorced years ago, and I never remarried."

"I'm so sorry to hear that," Kat said in a soft voice.

Dennis turned toward Kat and put his hand on hers. "It wasn't meant to be. How is your mom doing? I haven't seen her in years."

Kat cleared her throat. "I'm so sorry to tell you, but she passed away recently. This was her house."

He froze, and his eyes glazed over. "I'm so sorry. I had no idea." He looked away, as if trying to keep it together emotionally.

"It's a beautiful home," Rachel said, to lighten the mood.

Dennis nodded. "I remember this house was where your mother grew up. Her parents planned on making it into a B&B many years ago, but never got the chance. It was your grandmother's dream." He smiled at the memory.

"I had no idea. My mom never told me that."

Rachel stood up. "Ethan, would you mind taking Rachel and I on a tour of the house, and show us the lake? If Kat doesn't mind."

"I can take you," Kat said, standing up.

"No, you and dad need to catch up. Emma, you want to come with us?"

Emma stood and followed them outside.

"We'll be back," Ethan said, and Kat nodded in gratitude.

Thirty-Three

Kat

"I think she wants us to bond and knows it may be hard to talk about your mom with her here. It isn't, though. She knows how I never stopped loving your mom."

Kat took Rachel's spot across from him so she could see him better. "Can I ask why?"

"Excuse me?"

"My mom wasn't exactly a kind person. I found her journal after she died, and it seemed like you were the only person she ever loved. I want to know what she was like. How she treated someone she loved."

He sat forward on the couch, his hands folded together in his lap.

"Your mother was happy and sassy and also very guarded. Once she found out she was pregnant, she cut me out of her life, insisting you weren't mine. I had a feeling you were mine, and she was trying to protect me, but every time I asked, she'd get angrier and more dismissive." He shook his head. "Your mom came to visit me many times at the U of M. She would brag so much about you, but said she didn't trust herself alone with you due to her mental health struggles."

She still did not understand.

"Your mom was manic and restless. She would call me, talking so fast I could hardly understand her. She was excited and would go on and on with all these ideas of things she wanted to do for you and then the next minute she'd be having hallucinations and show up on campus with black eyes and throwing horrible accusations at me. She would even call me in the middle of the night saying things like you crawled into bed with her during a lightning storm, and she almost pushed you off the bed because she thought you were there to kill her."

The night her mother started locking her door and not letting her in. It all made sense.

"What did you say?"

"I called your grandmother and your mother was committed twice. She became too much for me to handle. I didn't know how to help her and she was suicidal. I called your aunt, and she supported my decision and promised me you weren't mine. She also promised she would be there for you if your grandmother couldn't be."

"Did you ever meet me back then?"

He smiled. "Quite a few times when you were like three or four. I'd come visit."

"How old was I when you had to call it quits with my mother?"

"Probably five or six. If I'd had only known." He sighed and shook his head. "I always had my suspicions."

Kat nodded.

"I know your mom wasn't perfect, but she did as the best she could with you. That I know."

Her mother's behavior was making more sense after talking to her father. "Thank you. For the first time in my life, I like I can maybe forgive her for the way she acted."

He put his hand on her knee and smiled. "I'm so sorry the two of you didn't get along. I hope you can be open to having us in your life. I want to get to know you."

Kat nodded. "I'd like that, Dad."

"Now, I've been dying to ask," he said, leaning in close to her. "Is Ethan the Elizabeth Conrad?"

Talk about an unbelievable situation. The man she loved her whole life also happened to be not only her favorite author, but one of her mother's favorites by the looks of her bookshelf. Her mother bought every Elizabeth Conrad book. She laughed out loud.

"Yes. It's crazy, right?"

"Do you think he'd sign a book for me?"

She smiled. "I know he would."

After everyone left, she walked with Ethan and Emma down to Lyndsey's house.

Lyndsey greeted them all with a hug. "Everyone is out back having a bonfire. We did not know you were coming, so you'll be a big surprise," she said to Emma. "They will be thrilled to find out you're Ethan and Kat's daughter. They all love you."

"Do any of them know you guys have a daughter?" Emma said.

"Just Lyndsey," Kat said.

Ethan shifted on his feet. "And Kevin and Brad."

Kat narrowed her eyes. "Seriously, Ethan? You told Kevin and Brad?"

He shrugged. "I needed to tell someone, and Andy kind of told Brad. It's a long story."

Emma grabbed Kat's hand as they walked up to the circle of chairs around the bonfire.

"I hope you guys don't mind,'1 but Ethan and I brought our daughter."

They all got to their feet and Kevin, Brad, and Lyndsey clapped and said congratulations, while Maddy, Whitney, Josh, Troy, and Victoria just stared at them in shock.

Maddy's mouth hung open. "Emma's your daughter? You guys have a daughter?"

"No freaking way," Troy said, exchanging confused glances with Victoria.

"I finally get to meet my niece," Victoria said, hopping to her feet and hugging her tight.

"You knew?" Troy said. "Am I the last to know?"

Victoria shrugged her shoulders. "Not my secret to tell."

"You look just like your mother. How are you taking all this?" Brad said.

Emma blushed. "Who knew my mom was this beautiful cities girl and my dad was a famous author? The only thing I don't know is why you got arrested," she said, turning toward him.

"Total misunderstanding. I'll tell you about it another time," he said with a laugh.

They all nodded.

"I've been keeping my mouth shut for far too long. It's great to meet you, Ms. Conrad," Kevin said as he stepped forward to shake Emma's hand.

"You have?" Lyndsey said, a confused look on her face.

"Don't listen to her, she's known for a quite a while herself," Kat said, trying to avoid an argument.

Lyndsey ran at Kevin and jumped as he caught her in the air, and she wrapped her legs around his waist with a high-pitched laugh.

"You can sure keep a secret, sheriff. Good to know."

"Same to you, Ms. Jones," he said, and kissed her.

Brad shook his head and looked away. "Get a room. Disgusting. Don't you know your brother is right here?"

"I can't believe this day. Ethan is a famous author. Emma found her biological parents, who happen to be my best friends, and Victoria and Troy are back."

Ethan hugged his sister. "You two are sure quiet over there."

They looked at each other and forced a smile. The tension could be cut with a knife.

Maddy frowned. "Is everything okay?"

Victoria's tears caught everyone's attention. "We have something to tell you guys. The real reason we moved back."

Ethan called out, "You're pregnant?"

Victoria shook her head and swallowed. "I really hate to ruin all this great news today. Maybe we should wait."

Lyndsey stood up and held Victoria's hand. "What is it? What happened?"

Kevin looked at Troy with a confused expression. "Troy? Please."

He nodded and grabbed his wife's hand in his and kissed it.

"Victoria has breast cancer," he muttered.

Everyone was quiet. The only sound was the crackling of the fire.

Ethan hugged his sister and pulled away gently, as if he was going to break her. "Tell me what that means, Tori. Are you going to be okay?"

"Yes, she's going to be okay," Troy said for her. "She's starting chemo next Tuesday, so we can fight this thing."

Victoria forced a smile through her tears to reassure everyone. "The doctors think they caught it in time, but I still have to go through chemo and radiation."

"Oh, Tori. I'm so sorry," Lyndsey said, hugging her.

Everyone grew silent as they processed the news. They took turns giving both Victoria and Troy a hug.

"I was hoping someone would take us out boating this weekend," Victoria said. "Maybe we could not talk about it until Tuesday. Just have a fun weekend celebrating being together, all of us, again."

"That sounds like a wonderful idea," Kat said in a soft voice.

Lyndsey looked at her brother. "Brad, I think you should take the pontoon out so we have room for everyone."

"I'd love to. Who's bringing the alcohol?" he said, trying to lighten the mood.

"Who isn't, is the question," Kevin said, and they all laughed.

They tried to keep the night upbeat, but the news was like a blanket of smoke smothering the fire.

Kat could not imagine how hard it was for Ethan. This was his sister and not one person there knew if she'd make it through.

Not much later, they all left, one by one. When Ethan announced he was leaving, Kat followed him out. Emma had already left with Whitney and Josh, and Troy and Victoria were helping Lyndsey put out the fire before they left.

"Hey, Ethan?" Kat said from behind him.

He waited for her to catch up.

"I'm so sorry about your sister." She watched him closely to gauge how he was doing with the news.

He looked away and clenched his jaw. "Yeah, me too."

They walked up the hill. "I'm also really sorry for the letter."

"At this point, I'd be more surprised if you hadn't run, Kat."

"Ouch, okay, I deserved that." "I'm sorry. That was harsh."

"No, I deserved it. The truth is, I'm so scared of being hurt that I run away before anyone has the chance to leave me first. I guess my mom really screwed me up."

He held both her hands. "Kat, I love you, and I mean that. I want to be with you, but you have to stop running from me. You need to trust me."

She nodded.

"Trust that I can't breathe when you aren't around. I can't sleep, and I can't even write. Ask my agent."

She looked into his eyes. "Really?"

He swiped a piece of hair out of her face and held her chin. "Really. I told you it's Side Lake that helped me get my spark back, but it was really you. Every love story I write is about you. The way you make me feel, the person you make me become. I love you, Kat, and you need to see that and stop fighting it."

She nodded. "I love you, too, Ethan. I do."

"Take some time to think about it. If we get involved again, you need to be all in. I can't keep playing this game with you. That's not what love is about."

He kissed her softly, then turned and walked away until he disappeared into the night.

Thirty-Four

Ethan

They all met at Maddy and Brad's house at noon the next day. Maddy made sandwiches and brought a cooler of food and drinks. David sat in the captain's chair with his father, a big smile spread across his face.

Ethan sat down next to Victoria. "Hey sis, how are you feeling?"

She slapped his shoulder. "I'm not the sister that has cancer today. I'm the sister who supported you when you were a struggling author and kept your secret when you made the New York Times bestseller list. I'm the sister who moved back home and wants to know all about the sexual tension between you and your childhood sweetheart. Now spill it."

He laughed and looked around to make sure Kat was not near. "Shhh," he said, putting his finger to his lips.

She frowned. "It's not a secret. What are you so worried about?"

He leaned back. "I don't know. She runs every time we get close."

She pushed her hair back behind her ears. "She's scared, Ethan. You know what it's like to be scared. She's been through a lot."

"I know. I told her if she wants to be with me, she has to stop running. I want to spend the rest of my life with her."

She gave him a playful nudge. "And if she follows through?"

He looked up at the sky. "Then I'll be down on one knee in a heartbeat. I've never been surer about anything in my life."

"Then don't give up on her. When I found out I had cancer, it made me rethink my whole life. I know I want to spend the rest of my life with Troy. That hasn't changed, but we said we would never have kids. But if I make it through all of this, I want to have children with him. I can't imagine a life without little Finney's running around," she smiled.

"Wow. I never thought you would have kids. I'm happy for you and it's a great goal to look forward to when this is all over."

She grabbed a bottle of water out of the cooler. "I love my job, but I want to do something different now. I've traveled the world with the love of my life, and I've experienced so much. I'm ready to be with my friends and family. I can't wait to spend summers at the lake again, and I'm even looking forward to Minnesota winters too. I want to expand my creativity to keep busy."

He nodded. "What would you like to do?"

"I want to do some marketing or advertising. It's what I'm good at. I think it would be a pleasant distraction from the chemo and all the other stuff that comes with this stupid cancer."

"I think that sounds wonderful. Maybe you could help me out with some book stuff. I'll talk to Zoey."

She nodded. "That would be fun to work on your books."

He kissed her cheek and stood up to greet Kat and Emma.

The weather was perfect as they boated across the lakes and went through the channels.

"Time for some swimming," Brad said after a while. He stopped the boat, and they all jumped in the middle of the lake to cool down.

Troy stood on the side of the boat, ready to dive in. Victoria snuck up and pushed him in and then jumped in after him. Their laughter gave Ethan goosebumps. He knew it was a possibility he could lose his sister, but Tori was right. Today was for fun, not cancer. And he was not leaving the lake and going back to New York ever. This was home.

The sky was darkening when they docked the boat. They dropped Emma off at Pine Beach and then went back to West Sturgeon to drop off everyone else.

"What a day," Kat said, looking exhausted.

Ethan walked beside her. "It was great, wasn't it?"

"Yeah. It's so crazy having a grown-up daughter. I feel like my life is just beginning again. Would you mind helping me carry my stuff to the house? I have something I want to show you."

What was it she wanted to show him? "Of course."

She tensed up, but smiled at him. "First of all, I want you to know I've decided to stay."

He laughed. "In Side Lake? At your mom's house?"

"Yep," she said, not really saying which question she was answering.

Did he believe her? She changed her mind too often. Could he trust her?

"I thought it was too hard for you to live in the house with all the terrible memories."

"It is hard, but then I talked to my dad and he told me my grandmother's dream was to open up a bed-and-breakfast and I've decided, why not?"

He was impressed. That was a great idea. Maybe she was finally deciding to stay instead of running after all. "That's wonderful, Kat. That house would be perfect for a B&B. The layout couldn't be better."

Her eyes shone. "I know, right? I don't know a lot about creating a website and all that, but there is no better time to learn, I guess."

"Why don't you ask Victoria for help? That's exactly what she was hoping to do while she goes through this battle with cancer. She wants to do some marketing and you know she creates one heck of a website."

She thought about it only a second before she said, "That's brilliant, Ethan."

"You'll make her day."

"Are you kidding? Making a website and marketing was one of the things that worried me the most. I was also thinking about asking Emma if she wanted to help me run it."

He stopped walking and turned toward her. "That's a great idea, Kat. Sounds like you've been thinking about this for a while."

"I also talked to Andy."

He clenched his teeth together. "Yeah. And are you two getting back together?"

She laughed. "No way. I called and his new girlfriend answered."

"You can't be serious."

"I called to let him know I was coming to pick up my stuff, and she answered the phone. I was relieved to know he moved on."

"I'm not going to lie. I was a little nervous when we found that journal in your drawer."

"That's the other thing. He admitted he tore out a couple of pages and apologized. He's sending them in the mail. He actually seemed happy."

"Wow. I was not expecting that."

He followed her around her house and into her gazebo. "What are we doing in here?"

The room was filled with candles and a blanket lay in the middle of the floor with a picnic basket and some wine.

"Ethan, I've been in love with you my whole life, and I've been fighting the feelings I've hidden from you for far too long. I've been thinking so much about what you said, and I want you to know I'm ready to spend the rest of my life with you if you still want me to."

He blinked. Was this really happening?

"Kat, I couldn't imagine my life without you in it. Of course, I still want you. But why did you bring me here?"

"I thought we could have a pillow fight and a little picnic. Maybe you could sign a copy of one of my mom's favorite books you wrote. Can you imagine what she would say if she knew you were Elizabeth Conrad?"

"She'd probably burn all my books," he said with a loud laugh because they both knew it was true.

She winked. "They were her prized possessions, you know."

"How ironic."

He looked deep into her eyes and held her chin between his fingers. "You know what I think?"

"Maybe," she said, breathless.

"I think we should recreate the first time we made love. These are the same pillows, right?"

She picked one up and threw it in his face playfully.

He pretended to be hurt. "What was that for?"

She shrugged and then tossed another one at him. "Just trying to set the mood."

The Missing Journal Pages

Katrina,

If you are reading this letter, things didn't go so well for me. They say my heart is weak, and it's only a matter of time before my heart disease kills me. I always thought it would be my mind that killed me, but God had another plan. I thought about burning my journal and destroying all evidence of my past and the secrets I'm so ashamed of, but I have put you through enough in your life and you need to know the truth. I sent you away after we found out you were pregnant to punish me. It was my behavior that pushed you to want to punish me by acting out. I could have stopped it and been a better mother to you, but I was a coward that hid behind a bottle.

Getting pregnant young wasn't easy for either of us, but I had one thing you didn't. I had a mom who stood by me and supported me through the hardest time in my life. I was depressed and too weak to tell the man I loved that we had a child. Whether you decide to meet him or not, I put his name and address at the end of this letter so you can find him. You have a half-sister and even a niece that I hope you decide to meet, but it is your choice. Whatever choice you make, just remember I'm so damn proud of you. You turned out to be this gorgeous, successful woman and the real reason I stopped reaching out to you was because I knew if I stayed away, your life would be better.

Your daughter's name is Emma, and Mark and Amy from Pine Beach adopted her. Maybe you already know this, but if not, go get your girl. Don't let yourself have regrets like I've had. She is the spitting image of you and she's such a sweet girl. I hope that you find your family and love them dearly, because that is something I deprived you of. I was too stubborn to see all your dad really wanted was the truth. I know now it wasn't my place to deny him making the choice whether he wanted to be a part of your life or not. I know he would have chosen you. I'm sorry I denied you your father and I really hope you can find it in your heart to forgive me or your hatred for me will eat at you.

I hope you find the person you want to spend the rest of your life with and when you do, you'll know it. Never let him go when you do. I'm sorry for the mother I was and the struggles I've had. I love you and I'm sorry it took me until my death to apologize. I added the reading nook and ladder, hoping I'd get to show you it someday, but now it is yours. I know I can't buy your love or forgiveness, and I'm not trying to. I just want you to find happiness and I know Side Lake is who you are and where you will find it.

Love you always and forever,
Xx Mom

Acknowledgments

Thank you to the professionals that made this book possible, Shirley Fedorak, my proofreaders, and Kristin Bryant.

With a special thanks to my husband, Owen, and daughter, Alexis, for all your time reading my books and helping me find the plot holes before they go off to my editor. You guys are the best.

Thank you to my favorite lake town of Side Lake for all your love and support. Your appreciation means the world. Thank you to everyone that has supported me throughout the past seven years and seven books. Your love and support have touched my heart and helped me continue to write, even on the hardest days. I can't thank you enough.

Thank you to all my readers. Without you, I would never have the courage to keep going. Your support means the world.

Thank you to Kim Osterhoudt at Pine Beach Resort in Side Lake, for all your kindness and hospitality, and the many stories you shared with me about the lake. I was lucky enough to spend so much time there over the summer hanging out with everyone at the resort, boating, swimming, and joining their bonfires under the starry night sky. I can't wait to come out again soon. Thank you for all your hospitality Kim, I'm honored to call you my friend.

Thank you to the Side Lake Store and all the businesses that sell my books and invite me into their stores for signings. I appreciate you so much.

Lastly, thank you to my friends and family, and the

teachers that not only believed in me, but helped me to believe in myself. I appreciate you.

www.jenniferwaltersauthor.com to sign up for a monthly newsletter or to check out her books.

Also follow Jennifer on Facebook, Instagram or TikTok @Jenniferwaltersauthor

If you liked this book, please write a review online.

Thank you for reading.